Her Sweetest
REVENGE
2

Also by Saundra

Her Sweetest Revenge

Published by Kensington Publishing Corp.

Her Sweetest REVENGE 2

SAUNDRA

KENSINGTON PUBLISHING CORP.

www.kensingtonbooks.com

DAFINA BOOKS are published by

Kensington Publishing Corp.
119 West 40th Street
New York, NY 10018

All Kensington titles, imprints, and distributed lines are available at special quantity discounts for bulk purchases for sales promotion, premiums, fund-raising, and educational or institutional use.

Special book excerpts or customized printings can also be created to fit specific needs. For details, write or phone the office of the Kensington Sales Manager: Kensington Publishing Corp., 119 West 40th Street, New York, NY 10018. Attn. Sales Department. Phone: 1-800-221-2647.

Dafina and the Dafina logo Reg. U.S. Pat. & TM Off.

Published by arrangement with Delphine Publications.
Previously published as *Her Sweetest Revenge*. First trade paperback edition: August 2013.

ISBN-13: 978-1-61773-981-1
ISBN-10: 1-61773-981-2
First Kensington Trade Paperback Printing: November 2015

eISBN-13: 978-1-61773-982-8
eISBN-10: 1-61773-982-0
First Kensington Electronic Edition: November 2015

10 9 8 7 6 5 4 3 2 1

Printed in the United States of America

Her Sweetest Revenge 2 is dedicated to the one and only "Jaye," my husband. I dedicate this book to you because you have promoted *Her Sweetest Revenge* just as much as I have. Your dedication to my dream means a lot to me. Without your love and support this would be a lonely and tough journey. So this is my way of telling you THANKS. This book is dedicated to you. I LOVE YOU!!

Acknowledgments

I could not start this acknowledgment without acknowledging the one person who makes my talent and creativity possible. My God. Thank You for allowing me to share my gift and giving me the wisdom to go forward. Mom, thank you for supporting me, loving me, and watching the girls while I travel to promote my writing. It means a lot. Angie, aka my big sis, I gotta show you love for always being the first to read my material. Your honest feedback goes a long way, thanks. And sorry for stalking you to finish ASAP, LOL.

"Jaye," aka the hubby, or should I tell everyone your real name, LOL. You still going hard with the support; it proves we are one. Team you and me. Shout-outs to all my family and friends: you know who you are. I won't call names, this way I won't forget anyone. Thanks to my editor, Selena James, and the whole Kensington staff for all you do.

To my readers: This one is for you. I never intended to write a sequel to *Her Sweetest Revenge*, but as your requests came flooding in, I thought, why not. And I must say I truly enjoyed putting this together. So this one is for you all and I hope you enjoy it.

All right, readers, here you go.

Author
Saundra Jones
1 keystroke at a time

Chapter 1

Pop. Pop. Pop.

"Agh!" I screamed as the hot bullet that left Luscious's gun pierced my left shoulder. Grabbing my shoulder, I instantly felt the hot blood start dripping down my sleeve. But the thud of Luscious's body hitting the ground had my attention. Then Luscious disappeared and on the ground in his spot Monica lay covered in blood. "MONICA, MONICA!!" I yelled over and over.

"Mya!" I heard someone yelling my name, but my body was frozen in one spot. Panic set in as I tried to force myself toward Monica. "Mya," I heard my name again. I felt myself blacking out.

"Mya." I finally opened my eyes and realized it was Hood shaking me, calling my name. "Babe, it's only a dream again. You at home and safe. So is Monica." I looked around the room as I realized I was home in my bed. "Shit, I hate these dreams." I sat up then slightly, pushed my Donna Karan stitched quilt off me, and climbed out of the bed. Realizing I had interrupted Hood's sleep again, I apologized. "And I'm really sorry for waking you up with this shit again." I went into our master bathroom to wipe all the perspiration off my forehead that had built up while I was panicking in my dreaming.

"It's a'ight, you know I got you. Besides I'm 'bout to get up anyway. Gotta handle business." As usual, I could always count on

Hood to be supportive. No matter what. But I was sick of having
these dreams. It had been well over a year since Luscious had tried
to sneak up on me at Stylz by Design to take me out. He thought
he had me too, but his plan had failed when Monica came out of
nowhere and shot him in the back of the head, killing him instantly. I was lucky, because had it not been for my sister Monica,
I would be dead. Luscious did end up shooting me in the shoulder, but I recovered so fast it was like a pat on the back. To be
honest, the dreams were worse than getting shot.

The only regret I had about the whole incident was Monica
getting caught up in the middle. I hated that she now had murder
on her hands. Even worse, it was her daughter Imani's father that
she had killed. It was only a coincidence that she had even showed
up at the shop that morning. On her way to school she remembered she needed money. She later said that she had attempted to
call my cell but got no answer so she came because she knew that
was where I would be. As she pulled in, she happened to see Luscious, who she thought was dead, slip into my shop. Monica said
she knew he was up to something and without a second thought
she grabbed the .22 pistol that Hood had given her for protection
out of the glove compartment of her all-white 2012 Dodge
Charger. Just as she entered the back of the shop, she saw me running toward Luscious as he fired shots at me. So even though I regret her having to kill Imani's dad, I thank God that she did.

As I came out of the bathroom, Hood headed into our triple-
sized walk-in closet. "Well, since I'm up, would you like me to
make you some breakfast? A little eggs, bacon, maybe some hash
browns," I offered. There was no way I was going back to sleep. I
refused to close my eyes only to get a glimpse of Luscious. Hell no.
I would stay woke.

I had told Rochelle I was coming in late today since I stayed
over the night before, but what the heck, I might as well drag my
ass in. I could get an early start on inventory since I didn't have any
appointments scheduled. Even though I owned the shop, I still had
a few special clients. And for my services they paid top dollar.

"Nah, babe, I'm good. I'ma meet up with my people early this morning so I'll just grab some on the way." Hood walked into the bathroom as I plopped back down on the bed and quietly contemplated my next move. I decided a latte would do me good so I made the kitchen a part of my mission for the morning. Not soon after Hood left the house I jumped in the shower. An hour later I had searched through my closet and fished out a pair of white Vince tennis shorts with a black Helmut Lang tank. I completed the outfit with Alexander Wang ankle-strap sandals. I had to admit my new style was classic. I had put the Brewster Projects dressing behind me. At least a little bit—I still would represent from time to time. With not as much as one glance in the mirror, I concluded I was ready to head out.

Chapter 2

"What the hell you doing here?" Rochelle asked as I entered her booth area. While I was off healing from my gunshot wound, Rochelle had got into the routine of opening up the salon. Recently I started coming in more frequently, but I still hardly ever opened up. I really appreciated her taking on the big responsibility of the day-to-day operation of the salon. Not once had she complained.

"I couldn't sleep." I sat my white Burberry bag down on a counter near Rochelle's hair station. "Having that dream again," I revealed. I was having the dream so much lately it was becoming a constant factor in all of our lives.

"Hmmmph." Rochelle threw her head around as she bounced the ponytail I had done for her the day before. It was long and straight then swooped to the right side of her head with crispy shark fins in the front. It was bomb. She was wiping her station, getting ready for her first appointment. Rochelle had turned out to be one of my top stylists. She had graduated top of her class for hair. And I had to give it to her, her shit was tight. Her clients always left with huge smiles on their faces and an appointment scheduled for the next week. "Mya, I told you to stop eating before you go to bed. A full stomach only enhances horror dreams. And don't be worried about that nigga Luscious, his ass is dead, courtesy of Monica. So don't even trip." Rochelle threw her right hand into her right back pocket and placed one of her feet on the bottom of her salon chair.

"Girl, I ate about four hours before I went to bed. And I ain't worried about that nigga." I smacked my lips. "I just hate them damn dreams. Sometimes I feel like Luscious is still alive lurking around the corner. But I ain't scared. Just creeped out by the dreams, I guess." I hunched my shoulders.

"Well, he ain't around no corner lurking. He six feet deep. You saw the paramedics take his body out on a stretcher and don't forget they pronounced him dead at the scene. Now, all you gotta do is forget about him and I promise he will disappear from your dreams."

I sighed, considering what she said. Maybe she was right: I was holding on to Luscious because he was on my conscience. "Maybe you're right."

Just as I finished saying that, Trina, another one of my hair stylists, appeared. "What's up? Ready for the hair show in New York?" Trina grinned. Trina had been working for me going on two years. She was also a bad hair stylist. She was fierce when it came to short cuts. Which was the same way she wore her hair, and it fit her round, plump face perfectly. Trina was about five foot three with hazel brown deep-dish eyes, a pecan color skin tone, and she weighed every bit of 180 pounds, but it was mostly butt and hips. She was what the guys called thick and we called plump.

"Hell yeah, we ready." Rochelle got hyped. "You know I love New York. Party!" Rochelle sang.

"Is that all you ever think about?" I looked at Rochelle, already knowing what her answer would be.

"And you know it. They got some of the hottest clubs up there. I feel my ass shakin' just thinkin' about going."

Trina and I both laughed at Rochelle being her typical party-animal self.

"Well, you better get busy gettin' the paperwork together. You know it takes weeks to fully get prepared."

"I am so ahead of you. I got the paperwork already," Rochelle revealed. "I submitted the documents weeks ago. I received the officials last week." The look on Rochelle's face said she was proud of herself.

I smiled at her. "I guess you have been taking care of business." I had to give her credit, but I already knew she could do it.

Trina was equally hyped. She didn't mind going anywhere that would get her away from her psycho boyfriend. "I guess we New York bound then. But until then, I got clients. I'll see you two later." Trina turned on her heels and left.

"What does Todd think about you shaking your ass down in them New York clubs?" Todd was Rochelle's boyfriend. He was a schoolteacher, a real gentleman. At first Rochelle was into him, but I noticed she had not been talking about him a lot lately. Nor had I seen him.

Rochelle shot her head in my direction. "You tried it," she said, mimicking Tamar Braxton. "That nigga ain't my daddy. I wish he would say anything about me going out. He would get his damn feelings hurt quick." She was rolling her neck. I knew she was not lying. Rochelle did not play the control game with any man.

"Anyway, he has been gettin' on my nerves lately. He wanna be all serious all the time. Wanna be committed and all that. I feel like he pressuring me with that shit," she complained.

"What is so wrong with that, Rochelle? You been dating him for almost two years now. He loves Tiny. Why you trippin' like that?"

"Look, I know how he feels about me and I know he cares for Tiny." Rochelle rolled her eyes.

"Then what?"

Rochelle pondered my questions as she sat down in her chair and twirled around, then stopped, facing me. "I guess I ain't ready for that yet."

The look on her face showed why. The truth was Rochelle could not move forward with Todd because she was not completely over Li'l Lo. Rochelle was still in love with him.

"It's Li'l Lo. You miss him."

"Of course I do." A single tear slid down Rochelle's right cheek. "A lot." She wiped the tear from her face. Rochelle had cared deeply for Li'l Lo. They were living together and had even planned to get married.

I didn't know what to say, but I knew how she felt. I had lost my brother, Li'l Bo, that same year. It was a void that could not be filled. To keep from crying myself, I changed the subject to shopping. If we were going to New York, our outfit game had to be on point.

Chapter 3

After a long day at the salon I headed home. All I wanted to do was sit down, take a shower, and relax until Hood came in. As soon as I jumped out of the shower, I headed to the kitchen and popped open a bottle of Merlot. I grabbed the bottle and a wineglass and went into the den, where I turned on the TV. Searching the channels for something to watch, I stumbled on *Colombiana* on Starz. I loved that movie. Pouring my first taste of the Merlot, I sat back and relaxed. Before long I was asleep and the movie ended up watching me. I woke up to discover the movie had long gone off. Looking at the clock, I noticed it was two in the morning and still Hood had not come home yet.

I snatched up the Merlot bottle and the flute I had been drinking from and started toward the kitchen. That was when the front door clicked and Hood opened the door and strolled inside. I stood in the foyer and watched him as he came down the hallway. I hardly ever tripped when he came in late. When I married him, I knew his position. I was more than aware of what he did for a living. I did not want to interfere with that or have him out in the streets worried about me being upset with him while he was trying to handle his business. I understood that his mind needed to be clear so that he could focus, but I was getting tired of the late nights and the risks he was taking staying in the game. The game in Detroit was no joke. I knew all too well the consequences of an unfocused dope boy. I grew up with the consequences, so no one could tell me shit. I wanted better for us. Common sense told me we would never be the Cosbys, but we could have a good life. I was tired of waking up at one a.m. to find his side of the bed empty and worrying if his fate would be exactly that of Li'l Bo. Without uttering one word, I turned on my heel and continued toward the kitchen.

"Babe, don't be like that." Hood was on my heels begging. He knew I was upset.

Putting the top on the bottle, I turned and rinsed out my glass before putting it into the dishwasher.

"I'm sorry, I didn't mean to be out this long but a new business came up. . . ."

I cut him off. "Look, Hood, you know I don't trip about you working. I don't call you blowing you up trippin' and talkin' shit accusing you of hoes. I never do that, but you are married; you have been for two years now." I raised two fingers at him for show and tell. "At some point shit has got to change. I know you love this game or are invested. However you may wanna describe it, that's on you. But it cannot be forever. That's just unrealistic. You need to seriously think about gettin' out and I'm talkin' soon." We had had this discussion before, but I was even more convinced that it was the thing to do. Everyone knew the longer you stayed in the game, the harder it was to get out and the more you stood to lose. I had to make sure Hood remembered that. But I also recognize that, logically, it would not be easy for him to walk away.

"Babe, I hear you and I hate these long nights. Don't you think I would rather be in bed snuggled up to you than out in these mean-ass streets. But tonight I broke into a deal that should get me out the game. Once it's done I'm out." Hood showed me the cut-throat gesture. I was confused. What now? What new deal? Another reason for him to prolong his stay in the game. The look on his face begged me to understand. I wanted to believe him, but would not cave. He continued to explain.

"That is why I'm late tonight. We had this side deal we been working on for months that put us through to some work. I put Rob in charge to jump things off. He met these guys a while back and the deal was successful and now we in there." He was searching my facial expression for reassurance. "Babe, this is huge. I promise, after this I'm all yours." He was all grins with that statement. He wanted to convince me more than anything. Rob was one of his top workers. He had worked for Hood for years along with Hood's other right-hand man, Pablo. Pig, Hood's best friend who had been killed a few years back, had brought them in. Coming from the same block, they had been a part of Pig's crew when he was starting out alone. So Hood trusted them deeply, or maybe I should say he trusted them enough. Because since Pig's death, he never gave anyone his full back. Naturally, since I was his wife, I was the only one he trusted with his life. And I would murk any nigga or bitch who threatened that. I was down for him, but I wanted him. Fuck money and the dope game.

"Hood, I understand what you saying. But we don't need any more money. We have plenty. You have several million in the bank, we got the salon, and more importantly, we have each other. Now is the time for you to cut your ties. You don't need no deals. Turn it all over to Rob and Pablo, cut it loose, babe," I pleaded, hoping I was getting through to him. The expression on his face was blank; there was no answer for me.

He stepped closer to me, almost closing the gap separating us. "Everything you say is true. I agree with you." I smiled without intention. Finally, he was listening and it was the right choice, the only choice. And I was positive he would not regret this decision.

But suddenly the look in his eyes was no longer the response I was looking for. Without warning that look had disappeared. "I have to do this. The deal is already in place. I sealed it tonight." My heart dropped into my knees. I had given the speech too late; this was not about to end. It all was clear. More deals meant more obligation to the game. This meant more chances to get killed or go to prison, a cycle that never ends. Constantly watching your back and dodging the haters. Suddenly I felt tired. I needed sleep. Without another word, I stepped around Hood and headed to my bedroom, defeated.

Chapter 4

"Hey, come on in." Ma greeted me and Hood at the front door, giving us both a hug. We had come over to hang out and have dinner. With all of us having pretty busy schedules, we rarely got to spend time together anymore. Normally, we try to get together every couple of months or so, then go down to the prison to visit Dad. He liked it best when we all came at the same time. But we all had crazy schedules, especially mine; it was just complicated. Not to mention that ride was long as hell. It was worth it, though.

"Ummm, it smells good. It's my favorite, enchiladas, right?" I wiggled my nose around to sniff out the food. The aroma was overwhelming. I could hardly wait. My stomach instantly went into growl mode. She knew I loved her enchiladas—they were bomb, to say the least.

"Yep. And I hope you both brought your appetite. Because I been out shopping and slaving all day to make this." She looked happy to see us. Each time I saw my mother it still warmed my heart that she had been clean for two years. She was a totally different person with her own identity now. For so many years she had just been Lester's wife. Now she stood on her own two feet. I was so proud of her: now Monica and I had someone in our family we could look up to. After Li'l Bo was killed, I blamed her and her drug use for his untimely death. I felt if she had been there for him, he would have never turned to the streets. But deep down I knew she was not to blame, at least not for all of it. The truth was, Detroit had some mean-ass streets that could not wait to swallow the young and black whole. Shit was crazy like that in the D.

"There go my baby! Come to Auntie." Imani giggled when she saw my face. She was sitting on the floor playing with some toys. She had been walking for about four months. Slowly getting up, she strided over to me. I loved her so much. She was an identical twin to Monica; the only thing she had that reminded any of us of Luscious was his dark skin and bowed legs. I scooped her up into my arms and gave her a kiss.

After bouncing Imani up in the air for a couple of minutes while listening to Ma and Hood stand behind me having a conversation, I noticed Monica was nowhere in sight. This was noticeable because normally she is the first one you see when you come by, especially on the nights we get together to eat.

"Where Monica at?" I questioned, looking around. Curiosity got the best of me. So I just asked.

"She in her room," Ma replied, then continued her conversation with Hood.

Before I put her down, I gave Imani another hug and kiss. I decided to sneak up on Monica. But before I could act on it, Monica was approaching me and she wasn't alone. Standing behind her was a boy with long dreads on his head. His skin tone was that of a banana and he stood about five foot nine and weighed at least 170 pounds. He was a cutie. That I could not deny. But what the hell was he doing here? I'm sure that exact question was written all over my face and Monica read it right away. She smiled at me.

"What's up, sis? I thought I heard you guys come in. What's up, Hood?" Monica looked over me and greeted him. I turned to Ma to give her a "what the hell" glance but she dipped into the kitchen. She knew I would be throwed.

"Anthony, this is my badass sister, Mya. Didn't I tell you she was a hottie?" Monica looked at Anthony and winked her right eye. If she was trying to smooth me over, that would not be enough. "This is her husband, Hood." Monica finished introducing us still wearing a grin on her face.

"Hey." Anthony reached out to shake my hand. Then he hit Hood with a pound they are known for doing on the block.

I was still dumbfounded as I searched for some words. "Monica, can I speak to you for a minute, alone?" Without waiting for her answer, I grabbed Monica by the hand and all but pulled her into her bedroom.

"Who the hell is he? And why is he coming out of your room? Just because I don't live here anymore does not mean you can have guys in your room, Monica. You are only seventeen." I waved my hand in her face. For just a second I felt ridiculous. I was acting more like her mother than a sister.

I think Monica felt the same way because with the grin finally wiped off her face, she stared me down with her arms folded. "You are right about one thing, you don't live here anymore. As I recall, you got married and moved out, or did you forget?" She actually had the nerve to try and pop off.

"Hold up. I know you ain't talkin' shit." I got defensive. Because one thing I knew for sure: Monica was not crazy and she knew how I could get. I was always in the "I am the big sister and will whup your ass" mode.

"No, Mya." She rolled her eyes toward the ceiling, but produced a smile that calmed me. "Look, Mya, Anthony is just a friend. And he was not in my bedroom. He asked if he could use the bathroom. After showing him where it was, I went to my room to grab my earrings. So chill. You know I would not be tryin' to get busy while Ma and Imani right in the livin' room," she explained, and I thought she had a point. But I still would not let her off that easy.

"Well, since you two just friends, why is he here on family night?"

Monica sighed. She knew I was just being Mya. "Because I want you and Hood to meet him. We been kickin' it for a minute. Plus we been out on a couple of dates and to be honest, I'm really feelin' him. Besides, he is a hottie. Don't deny it." Monica grinned and nudged my shoulder.

I had to smile because she was so right. Even though I was looking at him sideways, I had noticed his good looks right away. "A'ight, I ain't gone lie, he cute as hell." I continued to grin, but turned serious again. "You be careful, though. Because you have Imani to think about, okay."

"I know, and she always comes first, you know that. Never second-guess it." I knew she meant it. Monica loved Imani to no end. She would lay her life down for her, I was certain of it. I decided to give her a break for now and reached out and gave her a big sisterly hug. I loved my family so much. We were all we had and we had to protect that. No one would come between us.

Monica and I found our way back into the living room where Hood and Anthony were now chopping it up. Ma was at the dining table putting Imani in her high chair, which meant it was time to eat. And I was hungry, so I could not wait. We all laughed and talked during dinner and the food was great; all in all, the night turned out okay. Anthony seemed like an okay dude. I found out that he was nineteen so he was a little older than Monica. He was from Florida, but had moved with his family to Detroit more than a year ago. I felt comfortable with his answers, but that was not enough. On our ride home I told Hood to keep an eye on him and to ask around town about him. Something told me he was a hustler. Detroit was crawling with them. I mean, let's face it, ain't much else here to do unless you gonna get a low-paying job or got a degree. And there was nothing about Anthony that read college. His swagger fit the quota of a bona fide hustler.

"Mya, let me tell you about Wynita last night." Rochelle smacked her lips. And since it was about her mom, Ms. Wynita, I knew the story was gone be wild. Ms. Wynita was no joke. "Now, she been bugging me about going to revival all week with her and

Tiny. Last night I said forget it, I'ma go because I been wantin' to get into church but just been too busy. So I get dressed because she says she gone swing by the house and pick us up. I had already told her I could drive, but she was like 'no I'ma pick you up, just sit tight.' You know how she is: I was not about to argue with her, so I say cool." Rochelle shrugged her shoulders.

"Girl, we get to revival, everythang was cool. The service was nice. I really enjoyed myself. After church one of her church members asked her for a ride home, which I was cool wit'. How about on the ride they gone decide they wanna stop by another church to attend their revival since it was going on later than theirs? I'm like, Momma it's late, so drop me and Tiny off at my place. She talkin' about I should just go with them. That is when I knew she was trippin'. I'm like, Momma I got to work early in the morning. I'm opening up the salon. So she dropped us off at the house. Mya, how about she gone call me at twelve o'clock at night cussing me out. Accusing me of making them miss the service. I'm like, what, do you know what time it is? I'm in the bed. She on the other end of the phone still screaming at me. Talkin' about don't ask her to pick me up for church no more. When she the one offered to pick me up. Hell, she damn near demanded."

I was laughing too hard listening to Rochelle tell her story. "Rochelle, you know Ms. Wynita ain't gone change. And she still be hoeing you every chance she get." I continued to laugh.

"Girl, she is off the chain. And you used to think your family was dysfunctional." Rochelle laughed. "How did dinner go last night with Ms. Marisa and Monica?" She changed the subject.

This I could not wait to tell her. "Well, dinner was fine but I got a little surprise named Anthony."

"What? Ms. Marisa got a new man?" Rochelle got hyped. And as usual, her assumption was way wrong.

"Hell, no." I sat up to tell her this story. I had been slumped back in my chair.

"Oh snap, you mean Monica got a new dude?"

"Yep. I get there and they coming out the back of the condo

like they coming from her room. And of course I quickly jumped to that conclusion."

"Don't tell me you cussed that damn dude out. Not her new man, Mya. 'Cause I know how you be trippin'." She always accuses me of overreacting when it comes to Monica. And maybe it is true, but she is my baby sister.

"Whatever." I threw my right hand up waving off Rochelle's comment. "But I wanted to," I admitted. "Anyway, Monica claim she had showed him to the bathroom, which was cool. My main concern was who was this nigga? And where in the hell did he come from out the damn blue?" I was still curious.

"Wait, what he look like?" I gave her an annoyed sigh then rolled my eyes. All she was concerned about was what he looked like.

"He cute, about five-nine, redbone with dreads. Nigga look just like a thug to me," I added.

"Ummmm, I can't wait to meet him. What Hood say?"

"Not much really, but he gone be checkin' him out, though. But Monica claim they just friends. And peep this: they been on some dates already. And not once has she ever mentioned him to me. We used to be close." I pouted. The fact that she held it from me made me sad. She always told me everything.

"Mya, you know why she didn't tell you. You too protective. She knows you gone question her decision." Rochelle never bit her tongue. She could always be counted on to keep it one hundred.

I knew what Rochelle was saying about my being protective was the truth, but I had to be. My family was my responsibility and I took that very seriously.

It was not my intention to smother Monica. "I just want to make sure that she is okay. She got Imani to think about and she needs to graduate. And the last thing she needs is to end up pregnant again." It angered me to even think that she would ruin her life.

I knew Rochelle understood me. She had dropped out of school when she got pregnant with Tiny. Those were hard times for her with Ms. Wynita working all the time. But Monica had stayed in school and was doing really good. She was on the honor roll and was really focused on her future. And I wanted her to remain that way. The last thing she needed at this point in her life was for some gangster to come around and cloud that vision for her. I would not allow that to happen. She had worked too hard.

"Don't worry, she will be fine." Rochelle pulled out a pack of Newport cigarettes even though she knew there was no smoking in this building. The girl never learned. I think she just liked to hear me fuss.

"What are you doing? You know you better get outside with that cancer stick," I joked. But she knew I meant it.

"Dang, I'm on my outside cigarette police." Rochelle got up with a smile on her face. "I'll be back in a minute. My next appointment is in twenty minutes." Almost forgetting her cell phone, she doubled back.

"A'ight, I'ma go in here and schedule me an appointment with Renee since you booked for the rest of the day. I cannot be going home to my man with my head looking like this." I checked out my hair in the mirror. To me it was a mess, but I'm sure it looked good to others. I had grown my hair back out from that short hair do I had like Kandi from the Real Housewives of Atlanta. I now wore it long with curls or straight like Porsha on the Real Housewives of Atlanta. Most days I wore it straight with no curls. It was easier to manage that way, but today I was feeling the curls. After setting up my appointment with Renee, I jumped into my silver 2012 Cadillac Escalade that I had picked up a few weeks earlier and headed over to Dugans Hotwings. They were located on the Morningside side of Detroit and had some of the best hot wings ever made. After picking up a one-hundred-piece and some fries, enough for all the girls at the salon, I headed back.

Chapter 5

Driving home from a long day at the salon, I started to yawn. I had done two heads before sitting down with Renee to get my own head done. And after eating some of the hot wings and fries I had picked up earlier from Dugans, I was tired. I could not wait to get home, shower, and jump in the bed. It would be at least another four hours before Hood came in. But as I pulled into my driveway I saw two vehicles parked outside. We owned eight vehicles ourselves. We had moved out to Ann Arbor, Michigan, into a seven-hundred-ninety-five-thousand-dollar, six-car garage home. It was a lovely home, although a bit too big for us, in my opinion. But I guess with all the cars we needed the space. However, the all-red Flying Spur Bentley and all-black Tahoe truck in the driveway did not belong to us.

Inside I heard loud voices all going at the same time, not arguing, but an intriguing conversation. I slammed the door loudly so that I could be heard coming in. By the time I started down the hall, Hood appeared. I gave him a look that clearly said, *What the hell is going on?*

Hood walked up to me and kissed me on the cheek. "Hey, babe."

Not saying anything, I just looked at him. He knew where I stood on niggas hanging out at our house.

"Sorry about the noise. I got some guys over I want you to meet. Come on in." Without giving me a chance to respond, because he knew it was a chance I would pop off, he grabbed me by my left hand and led me into the den. Inside I laid my eyes on Rob, Pablo, and three other guys that I had never before seen in my life. "Babe, this Dontae, Rico, and Silk." Hood pointed toward each of them. "This my wife, Mya." He then introduced me to them. They all spoke, including Rob and Pablo.

"Hi," I managed before turning and walking away. There was no way I could fake a smile. I wanted those unknown pushers out of my crib. I could not believe Hood had brought these niggas up in my house. He knew I did not play that shit. No meeting in my home. Rob and Pablo came over all the time, but they were Hood's friends. They played video games, watched football and basketball sometimes, but never came for business; not in my house. After grabbing a Diet Pepsi out of the fridge I went upstairs to my room.

Once in my room I thought about the guys Hood had just introduced me to. I had taken mental notes of all of them. Dontae was tall, about six foot three, with muscles. He was a deep dark chocolate color with a shaved head. Rico looked to be mixed Hispanic and black. He was tall also, about six foot one, but he was skinny with a mouth full of gold. I immediately concluded he was from the south. Silk was a little more peculiar. He was medium height, about five foot nine, medium built with a low fade haircut, and a mocha skin tone. He had this long cut on the right side of his face, which I'm sure he wore as a badge of honor. The cut appeared to have been there for a long time. Everything about all of them read dope game.

As I prepared to get into the shower, Hood entered the room. His company must have left. Upset, I could not keep quiet. I was ready to bitch.

"I know you ain't left them niggas in the den." I sucked my teeth.

"Nah, babe, you know better than that. They just left." Hood reached for the remote to the television in our room.

I turned to face him. "What were you thinkin' bringing them here? You know I don't like you having those types in my house!" I referred to Dontae, Rico, and Silk.

"Babe, I know, but this was a last-minute meeting. I had come by the crib to grab something when I got the call from Pablo. So I just told him to bring them out here. It was faster because everybody was in a rush and got somewhere to be. You know I wouldn't have 'em here if I had a choice."

"Look, Hood, don't bring that shit up in here where we lay our head. I don't give a fuck what the reason." I had to be clear.

"I know that, Mya. Just chill, a'ight, I got a lot riding on this. It's gone bring in some major money. But I'm sorry I brought them here and I hear what you sayin'." He attempted to apologize, but it only made me angrier. He already knew my position on money. We did not need any because we had plenty. Plus our house and cars were paid for. I was sick of hearing that. I raised both my hands to either side of my temples and rubbed them. I could feel a migraine coming on.

"Please don't say anything about money to me again. FUCK THAT!!" I yelled. I was really frustrated with this issue. The conversation was becoming old. To make matters worse, he was having meetings in our home, our safety net. "You need to get out, Hood. Point blank and fucking period. I could care less if you made another penny from the drug game. You have made your share; don't be greedy." I tried to calm down and change my tone. I didn't want to be pissed to make my point. "I'm your wife. I love you. And I just want what is best for us."

"I know, Mya. But this game has been my life for a long time. In a lot of ways it has been faithful to me. But I promised you I would think about it and I will."

"I hope so," I said before snatching up my sleeping clothes, which I had taken out to put on after my shower. I disappeared into my double-size Italian marble bathroom. Reaching into the medicine cabinet, I grabbed two Excedrin for my booming headache. The nature of our relationship was changing; we had never experienced this much disagreement. I did not like it at all. I loved Hood like crazy and I wanted it to remain that way. I did not want the dope game to pull us apart. I had tried my best to be realistic, to look at things from his side. But all I could see was destruction.

Chapter 6

Saturday night I decided to hit the club. The whole week had been full of uncertainty for me, but I knew exactly what would cure that: music and a drink along with my best friend. I decided to let the issues with Hood go for now and just let my hair down. Shit, before it turned gray at my young age. So I called Rochelle up. Of course all I had to say was the word *club* and she happily agreed. I called Hood to inform him of my plans for the night and he told me he would take care of it. That meant I would have VIP at its finest. And of course he would be there holding me down. Hood always made sure I had nothing less when I stepped off into the club. He kept a VIP room reserved just for occasions like this when I wanted to party. I never had to share the crowded club space with anyone. He made sure of that.

Hours later I had on my makeup and my hair was flawless, flowing down my back. My chosen outfit for the night was a bright poppy-colored draped mini dress by Gucci with a pair of Gucci platform pumps to match. Damn, I looked good, after parading around in my bathroom mirror for at least twenty minutes. I grabbed my keys to my all-white Range Rover and headed out. Rochelle and I pulled up to the club at the same time. It was like clockwork. With a huge grin on her face, she hopped out of her Lexus LS 460. Yeah, she was balling. Although Rochelle worked for me at the salon, which brought her a very good income, she had money in the bank from when Li'l Lo had been killed suddenly a few years ago. Rochelle was the only one who had access to his money. After giving his mom and his trifling baby momma some for his daughter, Rochelle had kept the rest for herself and put it into a bank account. Lately she had been thinking about getting her real estate license and possibly opening up her own practice. Either way she was straight.

Once inside the club, I felt like all eyes were on Rochelle and me. I was known for being the wife of the Height Squad leader Hood. That carried mad weight so everyone knew not to fuck with me. We made our way to VIP with no problem while at the same time feeling hype because, as usual, the DJ at the Ripple Turn was on fire. Future's "Turn on the Lights" was banging out the speakers. Hood got one glimpse of me and was in my space in seconds flat. Pulling me into him, he kissed me right on the lips. The gentleness of his touch made me weak in the knees. I blushed.

"Damn, babe, you look so good," he whispered while looking me deep in the eyes with a huge grin. I had him mesmerized. And he was killing that Guilty Gucci. He smelled so good I wanted to drown myself in it, but I behaved.

"You don't look too bad yourself." I flirted back then sealed it with a wink.

"So I see you and Rochelle 'bout to take over, right?" He grinned. He always joked that me and Rochelle stepped off in the club like we owned it. I had to admit that was no lie. Rochelle and I were both considered to be two of the baddest chicks Detroit had to offer.

"You better know it," Rochelle chimed from behind me. You never had to tell her that she was a ten. She knew it. To be totally honest, we both were conceited. But in a good way.

Hood looked at Rochelle and laughed. "Well, I'ma let y'all have this. You already know the bar stocked with whatever you want. So turn up."

"All right, babe, thank you." I smiled. Hood spoiled me rotten. I couldn't pray for a better man.

"No problem. You know I got ya. I'm about to go over here 'cause we 'bout to start them shots of Don Julio."

"Babe, not that tonight. You know you get too bent with that." I playfully pouted.

"Right, you niggas need to put that up 'cause you know y'all can't hang," Rochelle joked. She swore nobody could take shots like her. "Ain't nobody 'bout to carry y'all up out this club tonight."

"Aww, you got jokes." Hood smiled. "I'ma show you how we do," he vowed while walking away.

"Come on, let's grab a drink at the bar." I grabbed Rochelle's hand as she looked behind me, over in the direction Hood's crew was chilling.

"Girl, who is them dudes over there with Hood and Rob and them? Ain't never seen them before."

After telling the bartender what I wanted to drink, I turned to face Hood and the dudes Rochelle was referring to. I noticed they were the same three that were at my house the other night. I rolled my eyes.

"Hmmm, they some niggas he gone work wit' or some." I waved them off.

The bartender passed us our drinks. Rochelle had ordered a shot of Hennessey. She always had to go hard. Taking one gulp, she downed it and ordered another one right away. That chick was no joke.

"Damn, ma, slow down." I laughed. "We got all night. Don't you get crazy fast." Rochelle could get krunk and quick. Just as I said that, Hood called us over.

"Mya, bring Rochelle over here," he yelled over the music.

We strolled over to Hood and the crew, and trust I was in no hurry. After the guys spoke to me, Hood introduced them to Rochelle. I knew then that somebody in the crew wanted to meet her, but which one, I had no idea. Not long after Rochelle and I returned to the bar, the DJ turned up with Trey Songz and T.I.'s "Ladies N the Drinks" and we hit the VIP dance floor. Soon as the dance was over, Rochelle hit me with the news.

"I broke up with Todd today."

"What? Why?" I had to know.

"I just need to focus on me. He wanna be too serious. He talkin' marriage . . . family. I just can't right now."

"Are you sure this is what you want?" I had to talk loud because the music was on blast.

"Yeah . . . it is. To be honest, I feel better already. Like a huge weight been lifted off my shoulder. Trust me, I'm good." She gave me a reassuring smile.

I looked at her good to see if I saw any regret. At that very moment I didn't see any. But I was on Ciroc shot number four, so I'm not sure how clear my judgment was, but it seemed right. Hunching my shoulders, I gave her my blessing. "Well, I support whatever decision you make." No matter what, she always had my support. But I did like Todd. I thought he was good for her.

Rochelle smiled at me. "Thanks. It means a lot. But I always know you got my back."

"Anyway, forget all this negative talk, we came here to party," I reminded her. I didn't want nothing to ruin that.

From that point on, we did just that: We hit the dance floor for nonstop dancing. Eventually the DJ slowed it down. Hood scooped me up and I buried my face in his Guilty Gucci. After our dance I noticed that Rochelle was at the bar having a conversation with Dontae. I stepped away from VIP for a few minutes and went to the bathroom. On my way back I caught a glimpse of Anthony, Monica's new friend. Although I had only seen him once, I recognized exactly who he was. Those dreads were like a birthmark. I knew he was only nineteen so I figured he had used a fake ID to get in or he knew some of the high rollers at the club. He had a drink in his hand and everything. I was looking back at Anthony when I abruptly turned around and literally walked right into Silk, one of the dudes Hood was doing a deal with.

"Sorry," I apologized. I had not been paying attention to where I was walking, because I was spying on Anthony.

"Don't sweat it. It's all good." Smiling, he licked his lips. And that's that shit I don't like.

Without saying another word, I speed-walked all the way back to VIP. Something about that incident felt strange; it gave me goose bumps and not in a good way. I felt some type of way. But since I could not explain it, I shook it off. Back in VIP, Rochelle and Dontae were still having their one-on-one conversation. I guessed I would have to find out what was up with that later.

Grabbing another glass of Ciroc, I went over and sat with Hood as he mellowed out from all his Don Julio shots. Feeling like eyes were watching me, I looked up to find Silk sneaking stares at me—either that or I was fucked up. Either way, I called it a night. I had Hood walk Rochelle and me to our cars. I told him to meet me at the house. The night was over for me. I was straight.

Chapter 7

"Damn, Mya, we turnt up Saturday night. I was so hung over I slept all day yesterday. Shit, I called Wynita and told her she could keep Tiny all day if she wanted."

"So that's why I didn't hear from you yesterday." I forked some of the eggs I was eating. I had stopped by IHOP on the way in and picked up some breakfast. To be honest, I had slept in the day before myself. It had been pouring down rain all day and I knew the extra sleep would make me refreshed for the week so I took advantage. "I ended up resting all day, too. I had Hood pick me up some Chinese food for dinner. I took me a shower and ate. Before long I was out again like a light. Snoring."

"Well, we gone need it. We got mad appointments this week. Plus I got to take two of Renee's clients 'cause she needs to be off." Rochelle popped the top on a mini bottle of orange juice she was about to guzzle.

"I already know. I told Hood don't be expecting dinner none this week unless he plan on picking it up. 'Cause ain't no way I'ma be able to swing it. Shit, I'm exhausted just thinkin' about it."

"At least we got to party, though. We need to do it more often, Mya. We used to have fun like that all the time. Now, we turning into . . . Wynita, " Rochelle joked, but she was being real. We never partied anymore like we did in the past. It felt good to have some fun. All work and no play made for Ms. Wynita, like she had said.

"I know, right," I agreed. "But check this out: While we were at the club I went to the bathroom and guess who I saw?" I raise my right eyebrow at Rochelle like I expected her to answer me.

"Spit it out." Rochelle grinned. "You already know I ain't got a clue."

"Anthony's li'l ass."

"Mya, who in the hell is Anthony?" Rochelle looked as if she was lost.

"Anthony, the li'l nigga I was tellin' you that Monica messin' wit'. Dang, yo memory bad for you to be so young."

"Oh snap, him. Wait, I thought you said he was like nineteen or some."

"Yeah, he young, he probably had a fake ID, though. My thing is why he hangin' out in the club. I'm tellin' you he about that life. I just know it," I said matter-of-factly.

Rochelle was shaking her head. "Hmmm, ain't no tellin'. Was he hangin' wit' a crew?"

"Nah, I didn't see no crew around him. But I don't know . . . I just don't think he is good for Monica. I don't want her or Imani around this drug shit. And I especially don't want him bringin' that junk around my momma!" I stressed. The last thing I wanted to think about was my momma gettin' back on drugs. Our family could not survive that right now; we had come too far.

"Did you tell Monica you seen him club hoppin'?" Rochelle bit off the piece of bacon she had taken off my plate.

"Not yet. I didn't talk to her yesterday. But she got an appointment with me this morning so I'ma holla at her then."

"Good, just lay it on the line for her. I mean, what does she really know about old dude? 'Cause you already know all these niggas in Detroit wanna be the next kingpin. Especially the young ones."

"Speaking of kingpins, I saw you talking with Dontae. What was that all about?" I quizzed, even though I knew the answer.

"Girl, you already know he tryin' to hook up." The grin on Rochelle's face told me she was flattered. "And he cute too, ain't he?" Now she was trying to make me agree to something that she had already made up her mind about. I had been knowing her too long; she could not fool me.

"I agree he is cute," I admitted. "But..." Rochelle rolled her eyes because she knew that meant I was bringing the negative. I had to keep it real.

"But what, Mya?" She sighed. Annoyed.

"I just wanna say that he a dealer and I don't think you should get mixed up in that again. You know that life is a two-way street," I warned.

"I knew you would say that. But just calm down. All I wanna do is go out to eat. And maybe a little shopping...all on him, of course," Rochelle teased, but I knew she was serious. Dontae would be broke all in on one shopping spree if he was not careful. Rochelle was good at spending a man's money.

"Whatever. I just think you should not get involved. And how could you break up with a standup guy like Todd? Only to turn to a dealer who might be doing a bid next month." I shook my head in disappointment.

"Here we go with the Todd conversation." Rochelle gave me an annoyed sigh. Monica appeared around the corner.

"Hey," Monica spoke. Rochelle and I looked at her at the same time. The look on Rochelle's face was relief. Monica was there, so I could get on *her* case, which meant Rochelle would be out the hot seat.

"What's up, Miss Monica," Rochelle spoke up first.

"Hey, sis," I replied and closed up the Styrofoam container I was eating my IHOP breakfast from.

"So this is what you two do all day, gossip and eat?" Monica always had a sarcastic comment for us, but we knew it was love.

"Here you go with that." Rochelle laughed. "Always gotta start that ish."

"I know, right," I agreed. We all loved going back and forward.

"Don't come up in here talkin' shit, it is too early." I got up and threw my empty container in the trash.

"I hope you ready. I'm missing my first and second period class because I'm at the doctor." Monica grinned at her own lie. Instead of just telling the school she would be absent first and second period, she would lie to them and say she had some type of appointment. Just never a hair appointment, but that school was not stupid. They all knew I owned a hair salon. Not to mention when Monica finally showed up to class, her hair would be flawless and freshly done.

After heading over to my booth area, I washed Monica and sat her under the dryer. I had to tell her about Anthony. But I didn't want to seem like a nosy snitch or an overbearing big sister.

"So you know we went out this past weekend."

"Did you have fun?" Monica scrolled through her Twitter on her cell phone.

"You already know we did. Before I left, I saw Anthony," I quickly threw in. "I mean, he didn't see me or anything. I just happened to see him." Still scrolling through her phone, Monica never looked up after I made mention of Anthony. But one thing I knew for sure: She was not deaf.

"Monica." I paused briefly while finishing up her hair.

"What's up?" she asked casually.

"Did you hear what I said about Anthony?"

"Ummhmm, you said he was at the club the other night. But I already knew that."

"So you cool with that? Him being up in the club without you? Around all them thirsty hoes."

"Ah yeah." She hunched her shoulders as if what I was asking was ridiculous. "I ain't his wife, Mya." She replied a little too sarcastic for my taste. And it kinda pissed me off because she knew what I meant.

"Monica, are you sure Anthony only nineteen? And does he work or go to school?" I probed more now.

"Yes. He is nineteen, just like he told you at dinner. No, he is not working nor is he taking any college courses right now. Why... what's with the Anthony questionnaire?" I could see she was getting annoyed. And to be honest, I did not like her tone.

"Look, I just want to know what it is you know about this dude. Is he dealin' or not? Because you need to be careful of whom you bring around Imani. And especially Momma. She do not need to be around drugs, period. You of all people know that." I was tired of beating around the bush. This shit was simple.

"Dang, Mya. Why you always gotta be so suspicious? Why can't you just be happy for me? You treat me like I'm twelve."

"That is not true. I'm just worried about you guys' safety and Anthony remind me of Luscious." Now I didn't mean for that to come out of my mouth, but it had slipped. I hated to bring Luscious up when talking to her.

It was too late, though. I had officially pushed her button. Monica stood up. "That is what this about, ain't it? You know what, Mya? I can take care of myself and Imani. You need to mind your own damn business. Messin' with you I will be alone forever. Ain't it enough that Imani don't have her father?" Monica snatched the smock off that I had placed on her while she got her hair done. After throwing it in the chair and grabbing her pink-and-black Prada handbag, she stormed out. My heart dropped at her statement. I knew she secretly blamed me for Luscious's death. She had pulled that trigger to save my life. But I never planned to ruin her life. All I wanted was for my family to be safe. I wished she could understand that.

Chapter 8

After Monica stormed out of the shop, I prepared to meet up with Hood for lunch. Because most nights our conflicting schedules meant we would miss having dinner together, we would meet up every so often and have lunch together. Either I would get home in time to prepare it or he would prepare something before he left the house. Sometimes we even had a chef come in for a couple of weeks to prepare meals. But even then we still never seemed to get to eat them together. In my mind that just added to my list of reasons he needed to leave the game. Even if I didn't leave the salon until nine o'clock at night, I felt it was a reasonable time. But Hood's obligations kept him out until one, sometimes two in the morning. Our life needed a change.

"What's up, babe?" Hood greeted me with a kiss. He had actually made it to Champs, the downtown restaurant where we would be having lunch, before me. Normally I beat him.

"Hey." I set the Gucci bag that I was carrying in the booth and slid in beside it. "I see you got here before me." I smiled. "That is definitely a first."

"Yeah, I thought I would do something different like get here on time." He grinned. I loved when we were smiling at each other. I missed it being this way all the time.

"Did you order yet?" I noticed there were no menus on the table.

"No doubt and I got your fave. Wings, fries, and steamed broccoli."

He knew me like a book, another reason I loved him so much. "Thanks, babe, I'm hungry, too. I need a Coke like right now." I had started to feel weak; a Coke would shoot my sugar levels back on point. Then I would be straight until the food came.

"I already ordered it. The waitress should be bringing it." He winked at me with a grin.

Damn, my babe was on top of it. Had it not been for the uneasy feeling I was having knowing that Monica was upset with me, I would have been on cloud nine, but the incident with Monica was weighing on me. While I didn't regret the way I felt about Anthony, I didn't want to have my sister angry with me.

"Monica is upset with me," I released. I didn't want to spoil our lunch with the sad face, but I had to talk about it.

"Why? What happened?" The look on his face showed concern.

The waitress approached the table and handed me a Coke and Hood a glass of draft Bud Light.

"Thanks," I said to the waitress as she turned and walked away. "About Anthony. I didn't tell you the other night, but when I went to the bathroom at the club I saw him." I sucked Coke through my straw.

"Why you ain't tell me?"

"I don't know."

"Well, why Monica mad at you?"

"When she came into the salon today, I told her about it. I asked her a few more questions about him. You know I just wanted to clarify some things. But she got all defensive and shit. She stormed out. Even had the balls to tell me to mind my business." I kinda chuckled at that one—my little sister was growing up for real. I remembered when she and Li'l Bo would fight. I would get in between their spats, but who would get in between ours, since we no longer had a brother?

"You musta really pissed her off. Monica never gets mad at you." Hood lifted his mug and took a swallow of his beer.

"What have you been able to find out about Anthony?"

Hood looked at me and took another swallow of his beer. I knew right then that he didn't have any good news.

"What?" I was impatient. I wanted him to tell it to me straight. No chaser.

"He slangin'." I watched the words roll off his lips.

"I knew it." I hit the table with the flat part of my hand.

"It ain't nothing major, though. Just small-time hustlin', but I ain't found out who his connect is, though. But the li'l nigga hustlin' for sho."

I took another sip of my drink when really I wanted to jump up, go find Anthony, and tell his little skinny ass to stay away from my condo and my sister. Thankfully, I knew that was not a good idea. It would only drive a bigger wedge between Monica and me. Hood was paying close attention to my facial expressions. He knew I was upset.

"Look, I don't want you to worry about him, a'ight. I got this. So far I ain't get no bad dirt on li'l dude or nothin', but I promise I'ma keep an eye out on him and shit. I'll smoke his ass if he brings the wrong shit around the family. All I want you to do is chill out, though. You gotta let Monica make some of her own decisions and unfortunately, that includes picking who she mess wit'. I know you don't wanna hear that but it's true." He was right. I was just being stubborn and did not want to hear it.

I did not want to hear the words that had just come out of his mouth. I looked at him like he had a third eye and a nut growing out of his lip.

"So what you sayin', Hood? Let my sister end up dead like Li'l Bo? 'Cause if my memory serves me correctly, you told me to chill on him also. And we see firsthand what that got him." I kicked myself as soon as I shut my mouth. But he had pushed a button. My family was my soft spot, he knew that. I felt like shit because the look on Hood's face was pure hurt. He could not believe what I was implying.

"Damn, Mya, I didn't know you blamed me for Li'l Bo's death."

Taking in a deep breath, I apologized as I looked him in the eyes. "I'm sorry, I did not mean that. I'm just sayin' I have to be there for my sister. I have to be sure she is safe."

"And what, you think I don't care about her being safe?"

I hung my head for a few seconds, but looked back up to meet his gaze. "I know you care. I'm sorry, babe." I stood up, reached across the table, and kissed Hood full on the lips.

The waitress approached us with the food in her hands. After setting it on the table, she asked if we needed anything and left. Hood grabbed the ketchup and started putting it on the fries. As soon as he was done, we both reached for some and devoured them. They were bomb.

"I gotta make a run," he spilled as he bit into a hot wing. I was still going in on the fries but I paused. I hated when Hood went on these drug runs. I always felt he would not come back. Since Li'l Bo's death I didn't trust shit with the game. And these trips were one of the things I did not trust.

"When?" I was angry, but tried to conceal it.

"Tonight. I need to be there by tomorrow morning so I'ma catch a late flight. I'll be back in about two days."

Clearing my throat, I closed my eyes for one brief second. "Umm." I dropped the fry that I was holding back into the basket. Ketchup was on the tips of the two fingers that held the French fry. I grabbed a napkin to wipe my hands. "So where to this time?"

He knew I was mad. The look on his face told me he was reluctant to tell me. But what choice did he have? "New York."

"You know what, Hood? You love this dope game so much. You travel for it, you stay out late for it, shit, you even kill niggas for it. At some point I have to wonder do you love it more than me. Does it make good love to you? 'Cause if it does, you certainly are fucking the shit out of it." My voice rose a bit with the last statement. A few people turned around and looked, including our waitress, who was delivering some food at a table across from us. But at that moment I didn't give a fuck. Rolling my eyes, I grabbed my Gucci bag and walked out. I had to get out of his presence before I said something that I could not take back. Hood tried to call my name, but I kept stepping. I had better shit to do. I was out. New York . . . the moon . . . forget about it.

Chapter 9

After dropping Hood off at the airport the night before, I decided I needed some time to rest away from the salon. Since I had no scheduled appointments I decided to take the day off officially. After a good breakfast first thing in the morning, I did some laundry and hit the gym. I had stress I needed to release. The workout turned out to be just what I needed. I left the gym feeling like I had dropped ten pounds of stress. It reminded me that I needed to get back to it regularly. Staying in good health was a priority of mine and I wanted everything to stay tight and firm. There would be no plastic surgery for me. At home I had a room that was turned into a gym. It had an elliptical and a few other workout machines, but when I worked out at home alone I wasn't motivated. Instead of working out, I would find a good movie and a bucket of ice cream with Oreo cookies. So sad Rochelle and I would attempt to work out at my house, but we ended up talking more than working out. Just another reason why we both keep our gym memberships.

Think of the devil! Rochelle's number was lighting up on my cell phone. "Hello." I was still driving. I was on my way home from the gym. A hot shower would do me good. My muscles were on fire and I could really feel it when I reached for my phone. But it felt good.

"Bitch, where you been at? I been blowing you up since like one o'clock." Rochelle was being dramatic.

"I was at the gym. What's up?" I switched the phone to the speaker in my car so I wouldn't have to hold the phone while I balled down the interstate, as usual ignoring all speed signs.

"Well, since you played hooky at the salon today, you missed gossip."

I knew this was about to be juicy. Rochelle always had the hot topic. It could be as bad as somebody getting shot or as simple as somebody's baby daddy creeping. Whatever she was about to tell me, I knew it was off the chain 'cause her voice was hyped. I could not wait to hear it.

"So last night I decided to roll over to Go Comedy with Dontae. You know Hood's friend?" She asked me as if I had forgotten who Dontae was. Now that was a topic we could discuss, but I knew she did not wanna hear it.

"Yeah, I remember Dontae. So you going on official dates with this nigga now?" I got sarcastic.

"Mya, don't start that shit." She sighed. I also knew she was rolling her eyes because that was one of her favorite things to do. "I mean, he asked so I went. Anyways, he straight and I'm glad he called. I wanted to get out. All work and no play ain't no good in this chick's life."

"Hmmm," was my reply.

"Yo, look, let me tell you about what happened . . ." Rochelle paused like she was waiting on my confirmation.

"A'ight, go 'head." I decided to chill. Monica was already hot with me about Anthony. I didn't wanna piss Rochelle off, too.

"So I'm out last night chillin' with Dontae at Go Comedy. And you will never guess who walks in." The sound in Rochelle's voice let me know that I would never guess this person they saw. But shit, who? I racked my brain quickly, fishing for an answer. Nothing came to mind.

"Felicia!" Rochelle yelled on the other end. My mind felt like it jumped time. Out of all the people she could run into and she runs into Felicia, The Hoe of Detroit. I had not seen her in a long time. Felicia used to be Charlene's best friend. Charlene had been cool with Rochelle and me at first ever since we were young. Then she started bringing Felicia around. That's how we all started being in each other's company for so long. But after Rochelle kicked her ass and I busted her upside the head with a bottle, she had kept her distance. Let's face it, the bitch was smart.

"You ran into that tramp," I replied with a smirk on my face. I glanced in my rearview mirror.

"Hell yes, and can you believe this bitch was with Silk, Hood's other new acquaintance. And apparently Dontae invited them. Well, at least he says he invited Silk and his new girl, but he claimed not to know who the chick was."

"Wait a minute, you didn't tell Dontae about the fight and all that, did you?"

"Girl, hell no. But it did come up that we knew each other. Besides, I was too busy watching that hoe. Because I do not trust her." Rochelle popped her lips.

"I know that's real," I agreed. That hoe was thirsty and slick. She all but wore a sign that said, "Don't trust me, I'm a slut."

"Mya, she come up there acting like we best friends. At first I was just staring at this bitch like *really*. I know she can't be cool with me like that. 'Cause if someone had put the ass whupping on me that I put on her, I would be fighting they ass every time they come around."

"I know, right." I laughed, remembering how Rochelle had punched Felicia in the face. And I didn't feel sorry for her one bit. Being a hoe always got bitches in trouble. That night she should have kept her wandering eyes off Li'l Lo, simple as that.

"Girl, she got Silk nose wide open. He spending crazy money on that hoe, too. I'm telling you this is another Charlene and Pig type situation. And get this, she finally got some real tracks in her head. The hoe was rockin' Michael Kors like a motherfucker. You know she can't afford shit like that."

"I guess she think she the shit now." I chuckled.

"Girl, that bitch think she somebody the way she was swinging them tracks from left to right. Easy giveaway that her ass ain't use to shit. 'Cause I ain't forgot when her ass was busted. It ain't been that long ago. Remember when her ass got caught stealing clothes outa Target?" Damn, Rochelle had a good memory. I was screaming laughing.

"Rochelle, your ass is crazy." I couldn't stop laughing. "Well, at least you didn't have to whup her ass." I looked at it from the bright side.

"I know, right." Rochelle chuckled. "Hoes, I tell ya," Rochelle commented, referring to Felicia and then with a sigh dismissed the conversation.

I pulled into my driveway and parked behind one of my closed car garages.

"So what you about to get into?" Rochelle asked.

"Nothin' really, about to go in the house, take me a shower, and pop open a bag of this P.F. Chang's shrimp stir-fry."

"Damn, that sounds good. I ain't ate nothing since breakfast."

"Trust me, it will be. I'm exhausted and hungry." My stomach growled just thinkin' about it. That workout had burned my energy and all my breakfast. "What about you? You doing anything later?"

"Nah, me and Tiny just gone chill out and watch *SpongeBob*. Tonight is her night."

"A'ight bet. Call me later." I turned off my ignition.

As usual, Rochelle had entertained me on the phone all the way home. There was never a dull moment when talking with her. After hanging up with her, I went in the house and jumped straight into a bubble bath. My muscles were already feeling the after-effects of my workout so I decided to let them soak. I felt like a new person climbing out of my Pearl bathtub. I dried off, then moisturized my body with some Cashmere lotion I had purchased at Bath & Body Works and headed toward the kitchen feeling like a million bucks.

Opening up my stainless steel freezer-refrigerator, I fished out a frozen bag of P.F. Chang's stir-fry just like I had planned. I could not wait to get the taste in my mouth. While reaching for my stainless steel–clad stir-fry pan, the house phone started to ring. The sound of the phone ringing kind of unnerved me because my house phone never rang. This had better be important.

Setting the stir-fry pan down on my matching stainless steel stove, I reached for the telephone receiver. "Hello." I sounded annoyed on purpose. Everyone that I conversed with knew if they wanted to talk with me that they had to call my cell.

"Mya!!" The familiar voice yelled at me. My heart instantly started to beat rapidly. Something was wrong.

"Hood." I said his name then held my breath with instant worry.

"Yo, where you been? I been blowing your cell up for the past half hour."

I had forgotten my phone was in the room on our bed. When I made it into the house, my main focus had been the bathtub. Nothing else mattered at that moment, so I had tossed the phone and forgot all about. "I been in the shower," I answered him in an annoyed tone, hoping he would get to the point.

"Oh, well . . ." Hood paused. "Look I'ma be catching a flight back to the crib tonight. My flight gone arrive at ten. Be at the airport to pick me up."

"Tonight?" I asked. I was shocked. Something was definitely wrong. When Hood went on a trip for business he never cut it short. "Are you okay?" I needed to know.

"Babe, I'm fine, just be there. I gotta go." Before I could say anything else, he had hung up. I was left with a dial tone buzzing in my ear. He had mentioned he would be on the flight, but he never said anything about Rob. It was odd, but I knew that Rob left with him so they would return together. I decided not to contemplate it anymore. He would fill me in once he touched down. With the stir-fry pan sizzling, I opened the shrimp stir-fry bag and dumped all of its contents onto the heat.

Chapter 10

On my ride to the airport to pick up Hood, I had a lot of time to think about Monica. I realized that in spite of my growing concerns about her well-being she was becoming a woman. She was a mother and she took good care of Imani. A smile crept across my face as I thought about how Rochelle used to always tell me that Monica would someday make a good mom because of how good she was with Tiny. I never would have imagined my baby sister getting pregnant at fifteen. Nevertheless, Monica was doing a good job at raising Imani and I knew she would not let anything jeopardize that. Maybe it was time I cut her a little slack and treated her like the young woman she had become.

All of a sudden the normal flow of traffic on the interstate started to slow down almost to a halt. Something was going on, but I couldn't see what. The last thing I felt like doing was sitting on the interstate in backed-up traffic. "Damn." I hit the steering wheel. If they didn't hurry up, I would be late picking up Hood and Rob: Their plane would be landing in like fifteen minutes. I kept trying to veer just a little to the right of the cars in the front of me to see if I could tell what was going on. But so far no such luck; all I could see was red taillights and signal lights flashing from some cars who wanted to get over. Not that getting over would speed things up; all the lanes were at the same slow pace. I hated when impatient idiots tried to buck in traffic.

Thirty-five minutes later I pulled up to the curb at Detroit Metro Airport. I immediately saw Hood waiting. As soon as my white Ranger Rover completely stopped, Hood snatched the door open to the backseat.

"Damn, babe, why you late?" He threw his bags in.

"Traffic was backed up on the interstate." Hood slid into the truck beside me. The look on his face told me his mind was busy. Something was wrong. He shut the door and rubbed his forehead.

"Let's go," he ordered without making eye contact with me. I was confused.

"Hood, where Rob at?" My eyes roamed the front portion of the airport, not seeing Rob anywhere in sight. Rob had gone with him on the trip. A minute passed as I scanned the oncoming hustle of people going and coming out of the airport. No Rob. Hood finally turned and looked at me.

"Rob got killed."

"What?" I was dumbfounded. "What the hell happened, Hood?" I could not believe it. Rob was a good guy. His longtime on-and-off-again girlfriend, Leslie, had just had a baby. I knew she would be devastated.

"I . . . I don't know. Shit went wrong. I just don't know." Hood seemed in space for a minute. I reached out and hugged him tight and I silently thanked God that he had returned to me. It could have been Rob giving Leslie this same news about Hood or, worse, they could both be dead. Reluctantly I finally let him go as tears ran down my face.

"Babe, you have to tell Leslie." I tried to wipe at my tears.

"I know," Hood agreed. "She been blowing his phone up all day, but I didn't answer. I have to tell her in person so I turned his phone off. But not now. I need you to get me to the crib." Without asking any more questions, I threw the truck in drive. Hood pulled out his cell.

"Yo, Dontae, I just touched down. Get to my crib. Now," Hood yelled.

I drove eighty all the way to the crib. No sooner than Hood and I got inside the house, Dontae was banging on the front door.

I told Hood I was going to our room, but halfway there I stopped and eavesdropped.

"Yo, what's up?" Dontae spoke as soon as Hood let him in.

"Man, what the fuck y'all gone do!" Hood yelled. I knew he was pissed. "Them motherfuckers killed my dude. Somebody gone pay for this shit." Hood tried to keep his voice down this time.

"Look, man, I know. And don't worry, we got you. Silk and Rico on that shit right now. We don't know what the fuck happened. Everything was set and ready to go. I knew Silk or I should have gone with you." Dontae sounded like he was trying to explain. But one thing I knew for certain: Hood did not play when it came down to money or his crew.

"I don't give a fuck about that right now. They fucked up. Now, handle this shit ASAP or I will. Ain't nobody gone play me like this. No fuckin' body," he screamed.

"Yo, you took out some of them niggas, huh?"

"Hell yeah, I bodied three of them niggas. That shit was on New York news this morning," Hood confirmed.

"That's what's up." I heard Dontae chuckle.

"Naw, man, fuck that. I want all them niggas. Dead!" Hood was clear.

"A'ight, my nigga, we got you," Dontae responded. He said something else, but it was muffled so I didn't hear. The next thing I heard was Hood shutting the front door. I turned and headed back toward the den, where I knew he would be. Instead I found him going into the kitchen.

I almost felt like giving him the "get out of the game" speech that I was always stressing lately. But somehow I felt this was not the time. His partner and friend was gone. The last thing he needed was me in his ear nagging. Although it's times like this when my point really brings it all home. The game was a death trap or led to jail. Unfortunately, Rob had succumbed to the death of it. Now his son had no father, and on these mean streets of Detroit his son would need a father. How fucking sad; another tear slid down my face just thinking about it.

"You all right, babe?" I walked up behind Hood as he grabbed a bottled water out of the fridge.

Without saying a word and keeping his back turned to me, he shut the fridge. I knew he was hurting. "You know the bad part of this type of shit is it brings back old fucked-up memories. Memories of finding Pig shot to death. I'm a killer, Mya. Done seen many dead bodies and don't think about that shit twice. But Pig...I can't seem to get that shit off my mind, at least not like I would like to. And watching Rob get his fucking head blown off brings that shit back full blown."

I felt so bad for him. I knew the pain of death. I knew how he felt, but still I didn't know exactly what to do to comfort him. Words would not be enough. But the love for my man made me respond. I gently but tightly wrapped my arms around his waist. Hood was still facing the refrigerator. He reached out, opened the fridge back up, and placed the bottle of water back inside. All the while I still kept hold of his waist. Unexpectedly Hood turned around and cupped my entire face in his hands. He looked me in the eyes and without warning slid his tongue inside my mouth. We had been disagreeing so much lately that our sex life had sort of taken a back seat. I mean we still got busy, but not as much and not as passionately as we used to. So the taste of Hood's warm tongue in my mouth opened my entire body up. He gripped both of my butt cheeks and my middle went crazy thumping. I was on complete fire. I wanted him and I wanted him now.

Snatching at Hood's belt buckle, I kept up with his tongue kiss, meeting each one stroke by stroke. His pants hit the floor and his member was begging my pants to come down. My juices started to flow. I could feel it threatening to trickle outside my panties. I don't know when or how but Hood had unbuckled my pants and they were halfway down my legs. I stepped out of them and Hood picked me up and placed me on our marble countertop and entered me with so much gentle force I screamed out from complete pleasure. After several intense strokes we became one panting in exhaustion. Damn, I loved him. And in my ear he whispered to me, "I love you."

A couple of weeks had gone by since Rob had been buried, but the whole matter still left me shaken. Every time I thought about the fact that it could have been Hood I shuddered. But I tried my best not to think about it so much. I just thanked God that Hood was still with me and I prayed that it stayed that way. Leslie had been doing okay as far as I knew. Hood had met up with her and gave her about a million dollars for her and the baby. At first she would not take the money, saying that Rob had left them straight. Rob had made sure they had a nest egg put away, but Hood would not take no for an answer. Leslie was a good girl; she was in school and really trying to do something positive with her life. I respected her for that. I also still wanted to talk with her to give her my condolences. The funeral had been so packed and emotional, there was just no time. So I called her up to have a latte at Starbucks and she agreed.

With both of our guys working so close together in the past, she would go out with Rochelle and me, plus I had done her hair a few times. But when her relationship with Rob became rocky, she stopped coming around.

I made it to Starbucks before she did. I got a good window seat since the sun was shiny and bright. Not long after I sat down, I saw Leslie pull up in her black Audi with dark black tint and all-black rims. The car was on fire. She stepped out with a pair of Gucci shades on with her hair pulled back into a long straight ponytail that swung to the middle portion of her back. Leslie looked flawless. Weighing only about a hundred and twenty pounds and standing about five foot three, Leslie was a li'l bitty thing. She had that dark chocolate skin that glowed. Her attitude matched her also. I had never once seen her act ghetto. She was nice.

I stood up and gave her a huge hug when she reached the table I had chosen.

"Hey, Mya." Leslie spoke while we still embraced.

"Hey, Leslie." I had to control the tears. Just seeing her made me emotional. I thought about her and Rob's baby. "How you been?" I asked as our embrace ended.

"Good as can be expected." She smiled as we both sat down in chairs.

"Well, you look flawless as usual," I complimented with a smile.

"I try. You ain't lookin' too bad yourself," she said.

"Well, you know us top models do what we can," I joked. We both laughed for a moment.

"So you wanna get a latte or something?" I asked, then sipped from my cup. I had already ordered.

"Nah, I'm good."

"So how are things going with school and the baby?"

"Everything cool with school. I graduate next year and I'll be done." I could tell she was proud of that because a grin spread across her lips. "The baby doing good. I had to put him in day care, though. All of my classes are morning classes; when you're in nursing school none of the classes fit your schedule, you have to fit their schedules. It gets complicated. Rob used to keep the baby while I went to school so I never had to worry." As his name left her lips, a tear slid down her face. Just mentioning his name was hard for her.

"Look at me messing up my damn makeup." She picked up one of the napkins I had on the table and dabbed at the center of her eye. That was her attempt to catch the next tear before it fell.

"It's okay. Trust me, I understand." My heart ached for her.

"You know I don't mean to sound typical, but I warned him. I gave him such a hard time when it came to hustling. I tried to get him to understand that I knew it was hard for him to just walk away. But once the baby came, it was time for a change. I would not have it any other way. I could not have our son growing up watching his daddy sell drugs. He deserved better. That is why we kept breaking up..." She paused and started back dabbing at her eyes trying to control the tears, and the choking in her voice still betrayed her emotions. "It's really hard to just walk away from someone you love. So I kept breaking up with him, but my heart would bring me back. Hoping that he would finally realize that we were more important than his dope life." Listening to her was like hearing myself giving Hood this same speech. I mean, we didn't have any kids, but what about when that time came? Like Leslie, I refused to bring a child into a situation where drugs were involved.

"I know what you mean, Leslie. I grew up in a household where my father worked the streets. We lived the good life for so long that it is what Ma grew used to. But in the end my father ended up in prison and my mom strung out on drugs. So the outcome was worse than all the gifts we received beforehand. That life is useless. Here lately I have been trying to get Hood to understand this as well. But like your situation, it's a no-win situation."

Leslie shook her head, agreeing with me. It was nice to have someone understand how I felt. "I ain't gone lie; it's hard. You know most of these chicks out here are only with these dudes for the money, cars, gifts, or whatever they can get. So these guys are not used to a woman sayin' walk away. They're just thinkin' about getting money." I nodded my head to agree with her.

"But Mya, you can't give up your fight for your husband. You fight for some normalcy 'cause if you give in, he will fall victim to the street. I wish I had fought harder for Rob. Maybe...." Again her tears started and they were coming too fast for her to control. I handed her another napkin. "Thank you..." She paused again as if to think about her next sentence. "Maybe if I had fought harder, he would still be here." I did not like that statement: It made me think that she blamed herself. This was in no way her fault and she needed to understand that. She could no more have stopped Rob being killed than Rob could have. That shit just happened.

"Wait a minute. What happened to Rob is not your fault, Leslie. I hope you understand that." Without looking at me, she hung her head. "Leslie, come on now. You could not have controlled that. Not even Rob could have."

Finally, she raised her head. "I know, but I just can't help but think. The day before he left we argued. I told him that I was through with him and I was gone take the baby and move out of town. That hurt him so bad. He called me right before he got on the plane. I was still being a bitch so I would not answer his call. He begged me, Mya, I mean really begged me not to take his baby away. He promised to do whatever he could to make it better. He never said it, but I think he was willing to walk away to keep his son here. But I guess I will never know. That message was the last I ever heard from him."

By the time she told that story I was in tears. I felt so sad.

"You and Hood have a beautiful connection. I have seen you two together many times. And he loves you. Even Rob told me how much Hood adores you. I just came here to tell you to be there for him. I know it won't be easy, but you make him understand that this dope is a street ending in a dead end. You love him out of this game. And when you have given it all you got and you can't do no more, try that one last time."

After talking with Leslie I felt emotional, but like I had a purpose. She was right. I had to fight for Hood and I would try. I would give it all I had because I loved him beyond words and the last thing I wanted for him was death or prison. Shit, I could not even bear the thought.

Poor Leslie had a long way to go. After seeing her and sitting down and speaking with her, I knew she was nowhere near being okay. I also knew those Gucci shades were for a lot more than style. Because after she took them off it became very apparent that her eyes were constantly red from crying. But I also knew that in time she would be all right. She was a bright girl with goals and a future ahead of her. With the love of her son and her family she would get through it. They say that time heals all. I'm not so convinced about that, though. I say this because the death of my brother, Li'l Bo, still ached as if it had happened yesterday, and he had been killed two years ago. I'ma just say it. That pain never goes away. And that's real.

Chapter 11

"Hey Mom," I greeted her as soon as the door swung open. I had stopped by to pick up Imani. She would be spending the day with me and then sleeping over at my house. I loved getting her from time to time; it gave me quality time with my niece and I liked that. I adored her so much and spoiled her as much as I could. I didn't wanna spoil her with just gifts all of the time. I wanted to spend some time with her and create memories: Now that was precious.

"Mya, why do you always knock? Just use your key." Ma stood at the door looking at me with a smile on her face.

"No, I will knock first. I do not live here anymore. I shouldn't just bust in."

"Girl, you have been difficult all of your life. Come on in here." She motioned me in. Once inside, I didn't see Monica or Imani so I knew they had to be in the back. I decided to sit down in the living room.

"Monica in the back getting Imani ready. She was running behind today. She stayed after school to do a chemistry makeup test 'cause she missed school the other day. Imani wasn't feeling well."

"What's wrong with Imani?" I asked. No one had called me and told me she was sick.

"Oh just a little fever and she was having diarrhea. But she better now."

"Good." I was glad to hear that. I guess Monica was still upset with me. Normally she called and told me everything. But since our last conversation, she had not called me once. I had called yesterday to confirm I could still pick up Imani today. After saying yes, she had hung up.

"So what's up with Monica and Anthony? How often he come through?" I had to ask. Since Monica was pissed at me, I was in the dark when it came to her so-called relationship with Anthony.

"They all right, I guess. Monica never mentions him to me. But they go out to eat and to the movies. He just got a new car so he has been picking her up some mornings for school." She said like it was normal. I on the other hand thought it was stupid. And I'm sure it showed on my face.

"Why she can't drive her own car?" That damn car was brand new. The last thing she needed was to catch a ride.

Mom shrugged her shoulders. "Mya, I told you I don't know. And she can be moody when it comes to asking questions about that boy. So to keep from smacking her I leave it alone." Ma smacked her mouth. "You know that all of you are just like your daddy. Hot-tempered and ain't nobody got time for that." She waved me off.

"Ummm," I replied. I was not trying to hear her compare us to my daddy right now. I wanted to know about Anthony. "What type of whip he pushin'?" I had to know. And Ma could say what she wanted. But I knew that she knew 'cause sometimes she could be nosy, but in a slick way, though.

Marisa started snapping her fingers like it was on the tip of her tongue but she just couldn't remember. "One of them umm . . . you know. . . ." She rubbed her forehead. "Audi, that's what he pushin', a Audi. A brand new one at that. It's nice, too." Just like I thought. Now what unemployed, small-time nineteen-year-old trap boy could afford a whip like that? I knew one thing, though, that nigga better not bring heat to my family or he would deal with me.

Finally Monica appeared with Imani. The expression she wore on her face was bare. I could read no emotions. This was not my little sister.

"Hey, little miss Imani." I greeted my adorable niece. She was such a little doll. She was dressed in a pink and yellow Enyce shorts outfit. When she got close to me, I realized she had earrings in her ears. Monica had gotten her ears pierced. Without me.

"Awww, look at you, you got your ears pierced. Monica, why didn't you tell me? You knew I wanted to be with you when she got them pierced." I turned my attention on Monica. My feelings were hurt just a little.

Monica just stared at me like her lips had been glued together. I could not really believe she was still upset with me, especially over some dumb nigga. Pulling her eyes to the floor, she decided to answer me. "Well, we were at the mall and I just decided to do it. It ain't like it was planned."

"Did she cry?"

This time she looked aggravated, as if she was tired of my questions. "No," was all she said. I decided to ignore her stank attitude. I was not going to exchange words with her in front of Imani.

"Well, she looks like a little princess." I smiled at Imani. Then I turned toward Monica, and without a word she handed me Imani's overnight bag.

I reached for the bag. "Monica, I know you ain't still mad?" I sucked my teeth trying to be cool. Her attitude was slowly getting under my skin.

She twisted her lips. "Mad? Girl, please, ain't nobody mad at you." She all but rolled her eyes and folded her arms, then forced a smile on her face. But she couldn't fool me: I knew my sister and she was upset.

Tired of trying to be nice, I became modestly annoyed with her snappish attitude. I simply had had enough. "You know what, Monica, whatever." I reached down and gently picked up Imani, kissed her on the cheek, and turned to Ma and said bye. When I walked away, Monica also stomped off in the direction of her bedroom. Ma let out a sigh and I knew that she was annoyed with both of us. If we didn't get it together soon, she would intervene.

After getting Imani safely secured in the back of my Benz CLS550, we headed over to the hair salon.

"Looky, Looky." Pam came over and played with Imani's big cheeks. Imani smiled, but did not make a sound. Then Rochelle appeared out the back room.

"Is that Imani?" Rochelle beamed with her focus on Imani as she stepped farther into the room. "Hi, Imani." Rochelle came over and kissed Imani on the cheeks. "Mya, she getting so big. Walkin' and everything now. Look at you." Imani smiled, but still said nothing. She had decided to play the shy role.

"Yep. She been walkin' for a minute now. When I brought her here two months ago you were off."

"It's a shame I don't get to see her more," Rochelle complained.

"Imani, you not gone talk to your Auntie Rochelle?" Imani looked at me, then Rochelle, and shook her head no. We all started laughing.

"See, I told you last time about acting brand new with me," Rochelle joked.

"So I see we booked as usual." I could tell because the parking lot outside was jam-packed.

"Yep, all chairs are occupied for the rest of the day. Except mine," she confirmed.

"Where Trina at? I noticed her car was not outside when I pulled up."

"Oh, she called earlier and said she would be in late. She should be here soon, though." Rochelle filled me in while still playing with Imani.

"So all of her appointments are covered, right?"

"Yep. But tonight will be a late one for her. All her appointments were scheduled for late evening," Pam replied and sat down behind the computer.

Rochelle suggested, "Let's go back to my area. I need to clean up. My last one just left for the day, but I gotta start Trina's second client. I did Shelia for her earlier. But after that I am done for the day."

Once in the back, I put Imani down so that she could walk around. Rochelle handed her a cherry Blow Pop. Imani took off the wrapper and walked it over to me. Rochelle and I both smiled. She was growing up so fast. It was still hard for me to believe my baby sister was a mom. Having kids had never even crossed my mind so having Imani was a joy. I could spoil her like she was mine.

"Monica still mad at me about that bullshit."

"For real. Girl, I thought she would be over that by now. Y'all ain't work that out yet?"

"I guess not. I can't believe she still upset with me, though. It's like she likes him more than she respects my opinion." I shook my head in disappointment.

"But you know that ain't true. Monica respects the hell out of you. You two just gone have to sit down and talk about it, Mya. Monica loves you and you love her. She just feels like you always treatin' her like a child." I knew what Rochelle was saying was true. I had to be the older sister and make it right, but I would give Monica a while to cool off. 'Cause right now she was tripping.

"Hey." Trina strolled in with a pair of sunglasses on. That was strange because the one thing Trina was proud of were her big deep-dish eyes. So there was no way she was coming inside of a building with glasses on. Something was up.

"What's up," Rochelle and I spoke in unison then stared at each other while Trina made her way over to Imani and picked her up. She was crazy about Imani, too. Rochelle shook her head at me. We turned our attention back to Trina, who was indulged in Imani.

"I covered Shelia for you this morning. And yes, she was happy with my service." Rochelle was leading to something.

"Why wouldn't she be? You one of the baddest stylists here," Trina commented and continued to play with Imani. "And thanks.

I owe you. I knew you would take good care of her." Rochelle looked at me and twisted her lips. We both knew Trina was stalling. I hollered for Pam to come back and get Imani so that we could get to the bottom of the shades. As soon as Pam and Imani were out of the room, I went in.

"Are you okay? Rochelle told me you were coming in late today."

"Yeah, I'm fine. I just had some unexpected business to take care of. But everything is cool now," Trina answered.

"Cool," I replied, but I still wanted to know why she was wearing those sunglasses inside the building. I was already sick of beating around the bush. So fuck it. "Trina, why are you wearing sunglasses?"

Trina turned toward us with her lips curled into a smile. "Girl, can't you see they go with my outfit." She chuckled and I knew it was forced.

"Well, bitch, you must be blind 'cause them shades don't match nothin' you wearin'," Rochelle blurted out, being her normal, opinionated, say-what-was-on-her-mind self. I almost laughed, but instead I controlled it. I grunted, clearing my throat. then gave her the *shut-up* look.

I focused my attention back on Trina. "Trina, why do you have on the shades?" I asked again. "And this time give me a real answer, not some bullshit."

Still stalling, she did not answer me; she just stood glued to her spot. I could not see her eyes so I didn't know if she was looking at me or Rochelle. The shades were so dark I couldn't see her eyes period. A single tear slid down her left cheek and I knew that something was amiss. The shades had a meaning; slowly raising her right hand, Trina removed them. Rochelle and I both grabbed at our mouths to quiet our gasps. Trina's right eye was black and blue and completely swollen shut. Her long eyelashes were completely invisible. She did not have to say a word; we all knew who was responsible: Teddy, her deadbeat boyfriend.

Teddy was a loser with no job who nickel-and-dimed weed

sacks with a constant dream of being the next kingpin of Detroit, all while beating and controlling Trina. I had told her time and time again to leave him, and this time would be no different. I cursed under my breath and my heart broke a little bit more for Trina. I would never let some nigga beat me. I would kill him first because my daddy didn't raise no punching bag.

Chapter 12

"Aye babe, what you got planned for the day?" Hood yelled from the bathroom. I had just finished strapping up my Alexandre Birman leather thong sandals while watching Imani lie on the floor hugging her Pillow Pet pretending to be asleep. I had to smile at her, she was too cute. And way too smart for her age.

"Well, after I get Imani dropped off, I'ma meet Rochelle at Lace to get a mani and pedi. Why, what's up?"

"I was hoping we could catch up about five or six and grab some steaks at Outback Steakhouse and shit. We ain't been there in a minute and I been wanting to go. A nigga mouth is watering for a T-bone." Hood made sure he expressed T-bone with a raised eyebrow. I knew how much he loved a good steak and, now that he mentioned it, I wouldn't mind having one myself.

"A'ight, that's cool. I'll meet you there instead of coming all the way back to the house." Standing up, I walked over and started to tickle Imani. She rolled over with giggles. The doorbell rang and I knew it had to be Silk and Dontae. Hood had informed me over breakfast that they would be stopping by. They needed to discuss something important and it would only take a minute. He knew how I felt about having them at my house, but he assured me that there would be no drug activity. The only reason he had agreed to let them stop by was because they would be in the area and would be catching a plane for a quick trip right after.

"Hood, the doorbell ringing, you need to get that." I yelled so that he could hear me over the shower water that was running. I got no answer so I yelled louder. "Hood, you need to get the door. You know it's for you," I added sarcastically. He knew I did not want to answer the door for his clown homies.

"I'm still in the shower," he yelled back so that I could hear him. "Can you get it for me, babe, and tell them niggas to chill until I'm done. I'll be out in a minute."

"Ugh," I sighed out loud then rolled my eyes. Imani looked at me and giggled. I'm sure she thought my facial expression was funny. But I was annoyed because Hood knew I didn't wanna let them niggas in my house. If it was up to me, they would stand outside until he was out of the shower. The more I thought about it, that sounded like a good idea. But I knew that was mean.

I headed to the front door with Imani on my trail holding her black-and-yellow bumblebee Pillow Pet. I didn't want to be rude so I tried to wipe the frown off my face, but there was no way I would smile. Hell no. I refused.

I swung open the front door to only find Silk standing there gawking at me. I just wanted to slam the door in his face. And where was his fake-ass friend Dontae? "Ain't there supposed to be two of you?" I stuck my head outside the door and looked around, but there was only Silk, no sign of Dontae.

"Yeah, but Dontae running late. I'm here, though. Hood up in there?" Silk had a look on his face like I was blocking his view. I know his ass was not in a hurry to get up in my crib. I had to control myself because I almost rolled my eyes at his impatient ass.

"Come on in." I turned around and headed down the hallway. Imani had stopped midway in the hall and was trying to look around me to see Silk. Looking up at me with her big eyes, Imani asked me in her two-year-old voice to pick her up. She held out her arms and her Pillow Pet to me.

"She really cute." Silk's voice broke my thoughts. For a second I had forgotten he was there. "And she looks just like you." I watched Silk as a wide smile grew across his face.

"She's my niece. I guess it's genetics." It was the only polite thing I could think of at that moment. The smile on his face was plastered there except there was another look in his eyes. He glared at me in a way that gave me the creeps. I almost shuddered. There was something about him I didn't like. He made me feel as if I was being watched and I didn't like it one bit.

"Well, you can have a seat in the den. Hood will be out in a minute." I pointed toward the den area so that he could lead himself. He had been in there before so I was confident he would not get lost. I scooped Imani up and made a dash for my bedroom. Hood was sliding into a pair of navy blue and white high-top Adidas when I entered the room.

"Them niggas straight?" He glanced up at me for a second then back at the Adidas.

"Ain't no 'them niggas,' Silk is alone," I confirmed, then sat Imani on my bed. Hood briefly looked up at me again but continued to get his Adidas on.

"Silk says Dontae is running late." I twisted up my lips as I swished into my huge walk-in closet. I grabbed my tan Michael Kors handbag. Hood was putting on his Gucci G Chrono watch when I exited the closet.

"Look, I don't want them niggas back in here. I don't care what it's for. Got it?" My attitude kicked in. I wanted to make myself clear.

"A'ight." Hood looked at me. He knew me and knew that something was bothering me. "What's up? Why you so emotional about that shit?"

"Nothing but that nigga Silk creeps me out. I don't like him." I had to be honest. That nigga Silk made me feel uncomfortable in my own home.

Hood immediately stopped messing with his watch and a killer look graced his face. "That nigga say some outa line to you? Tell me now 'cause I'll go down there and dead that nigga ASAP!" Hood barked. I knew he meant it.

"Hood, keep your voice down." I tried to calm him.

"Fuck that shit, Mya." Hood turned to leave the room. I ran in front of him. I knew this could turn bad quick. I didn't mean to flip him out.

"Hood, stop, babe, it's not like that." I blocked the door. "All I'm saying is the guy creeps me out. He has not said anything out of line to me. Besides, you know if he did that, I would snap out on him myself," I reminded him. He knew I could hold my own.

Hood kept his eyes glued on me. I knew he was ready to buck. Poor Silk sitting in the den had no idea how close he had just come to death. "You sure?"

"Yes, babe, now chill. Just keep them out of our house. Okay? No more business conversations here, period." I looked him in the eyes.

"No doubt." He stroked my face and kissed me deeply on the lips.

"Imani," I said and Hood moved out the way. I had completely forgotten she was in the room, she was so quiet. The last thing I wanted to do was frighten her. But when I looked over, she was sleeping. That's why she had wanted me to pick her up, she was sleepy. Smiling at her, I told Hood to pull my silver Escalade out of the garage. I would carry Imani out and strap her into her car seat. I refused to wake her from her toddler beauty sleep. And on the other hand, I had to get out in the fresh air. My day was already starting to be chaotic. Hood did not play that shit. You mess with his woman and your ass would end up in a body bag. I smiled at how hard I knew my man went when it came to me, but I didn't want him killing niggas if I could help it.

Chapter 13

After I dropped Imani off, Rochelle called me to cancel our prior plan to meet up at Lace. Apparently Pam could not make her shift at the salon and the only other people that could cover were Rochelle or me. But since I had given Rochelle so much responsibility, she normally would take care of these situations when they arose. As much as I wanted to get my mani and pedi, I also wanted to hang out with Rochelle. So instead of heading to Lace, I took a detour and headed straight to the salon. Pulling up to the salon, I noticed that Rochelle's Lexus was not outside, which was odd. I had just hung up with her about ten minutes before and she said she was at the salon. I pulled into my reserved parking space and I hopped out, hit the alarm, and strutted my way inside my establishment.

Once inside, I saw Rochelle sitting at the receptionist desk. She had just scheduled an appointment and was hanging up the phone.

"What's up, chick?" Rochelle greeted me, popping her chewing gum.

"Ahh, do you know that your car ain't outside." I flipped my hair off my shoulder while balancing my Michael Kors bag on my right wrist.

"Yeah, I know. It's parked at my house. I was chauffeured to work this morning." Rochelle grinned and flashed her Colgate white teeth. I knew it was some nigga and it had nothing to do with Todd.

Without saying a word, Rochelle continued to grin at me. I was growing impatient. I shifted my weight from my left side to the right. She knew I wanted to know who had dropped her off at work. "Bitch, spill the beans. Who is it?" I could no longer wait.

"I went out with Dontae last night. I ended up spending the night with him. He was just dropping me off at home when I got the call from Pam. Long story short, I asked him if he could drop me off at work and he agreed." She shrugged her shoulders, still holding on to that smile.

I guess that was the reason Dontae was running late meeting with Hood this morning. "Damn, can you wipe that smile off your face?" I rolled my eyes.

"See, I knew you would trip. That is why I did not tell you on the phone," Rochelle accused me. She knew how I felt about her dating another dope boy.

Sucking my teeth, I denied it. "I ain't trippin' if that's what you wanna do. That is your business."

All of a sudden the smile on Rochelle's face disappeared as she seemed to think about something. Before I could ask, she looked at me. "Wynita already trippin'. She called me this mornin' when I didn't pick up Tiny. I tried to call her last night, but she was asleep so I left her a message telling her I would pick Tiny up this morning. Girl, she couldn't wait to call me first thing this morning talkin' shit. Since Dontae was around, I told her I would call her back. By the time I made it here, she was calling me again. Screaming I need to get rid of Dontae because she know he ain't nothing but bad news."

"Well, I agree with her, but that's just my feelings on the situation."

"But, Mya, he a sweetie and cool as fuck. You know I like that type of shit."

"You just looking for another Li'l Lo." That was some truth for her ass. But I figured she would deny it. Typical.

"Hell no, he ain't nothing like Li'l Lo. I will never find another love like him. That was my boo." Talking about Li'l Lo was a soft spot with Rochelle, so I decided to chill on that.

"It's all good, though. Do you." Just as we were squashing that conversation, Trina came up. Her face had healed up and she was back in her happy mode. Sadly enough, she was back with Teddy. He had apologized, just as he had a million times before, and she had forgiven him and gone home. While Rochelle had cursed her out and called her stupid, I silently prayed for her because I knew that this situation would end up bad if she didn't eventually get out. I also knew from experience that people did what they wanted to do until they had had enough. Trina's situation was no different. Calling her stupid was not going to change that. But telling Rochelle that was a waste of time.

"So have the tickets been booked for New York? 'Cause I'm ready to bounce." Trina smiled.

"Hell yeah, they booked. You just get packed. Shit, we gone turn up." Rochelle was equally hyped about the trip.

I was excited about the trip, too. I knew we were going to have lots of fun, not to mention shop till we dropped. "I'm ready, too," I admitted.

"Damn, and it's gone be fashion week, too. We gone be poppin' bottles like crazy." Rochelle stood up and smacked five with Trina. We were all laughing, then all of a sudden Rochelle looked toward the door and her smile faded. I immediately turned in the direction that Rochelle's eyes traveled and came face to face with the unexpected. Felicia. A bitch from our past, like I said before. But as of late she was popping up on Rochelle, now on me at my salon, so I guess she did not plan to keep it that way. You could always expect the unexpected from Charlene and Felicia, especially when it came to money. Because, to be honest, both of those bitches were gold diggers. Unfortunately, Felicia had not been as lucky when it came to finding a baller that was willing to settle down with her. Needless to say, in the Brewster her reputation preceded her. But lucky for her, Silk was not from Detroit. So he didn't know about her open legs to the Detroit community. Either way, I could care less about the bitch. If I never saw her again that would be too soon. And here she was standing in my salon. What the fuck did she want?

I had to admit, though, money was doing her good. In the past I had never seen her in no more than Baby Phat. Here she was standing in front of me in Burberry down with some Prada. And she brought her ego. It was riding shotgun on her shoulder. With a slight smile, she spoke to me and Rochelle by name. The hoe had nerves.

Instead of opening our mouths, we both nodded in her direction. Trina knew something was up, but had no clue as to what. She gave me and Rochelle a questionable look.

"I need to get my head done," Felicia spoke up again.

I was not shocked at her ghetto tact. See, you can put red bottoms on a bitch and she will still be hood. How she gone stroll her Brewster project ass up in a five-star hair salon thinkin' a chair was waiting for her and that old cheap-ass weave. I turned and looked at Rochelle, who grinned.

I turned back around to face Felicia. "Sweetie, this is a business, okay. Now what that means is you need an appointment to get your wig done up in here." I was being sarcastic, but I wanted to be clear.

Felicia turned around and looked at her hood-rat friend who she had brought along with her. This bitch had the nerve to blow a bubble with the wad of gum she was chewing on. Looking back at me, Felicia tried her plan B. "I know this a business." She scanned the reception area, shaking her head in approval. "By the way, it looks really nice. And I'm sure that a nice salon like this can fit me in. Besides, I can pay extra." Felicia dug inside her Burberry bag and pulled out a wad of money. Just like a hood rat to not have her money in a wallet. The bitch rockin' a seven-hundred-dollar bag with money just thrown inside. Ugh. I shook my head in disgust.

"Rochelle, look in the computer and tell her who and what

appointment times they may have available." I kept my eyes on Felicia, not impressed by her cash flashing.

The smile Felicia was rocking when she first entered the salon had now faded; she started to look defeated. Rochelle scrolled through the data on the computer looking for slots. It was taking a minute because we were normally so booked. New appointments most of the time ended up being a month out. Felicia started to shift her weight from left foot to right foot as she was growing impatient. I enjoyed that a lot.

"Looks like the first thing we have coming up is gone be at least four weeks away," Rochelle finally said.

"Are you sure? Because that is too fucking long." Felicia frowned.

"If that's what I said we got, then that's it. Now if you can't wait, why don't you go some fucking place else?" Rochelle shot back before I could stop her.

"What . . ." Felicia started to shout back. Trina stepped in.

"I'll do it for you. Right now." Since Trina was always fighting with Teddy in her daily home life, she was not big on drama.

"Trina, you don't have to . . ." I started to speak.

Trina looked at me with a reassured look. "I will do it. My next appointment is not for two hours. I came in early to work on a wig. So I can do it. Now, what's your name again?" Trina asked.

"Felicia." The bitch had the nerve to roll her eyes.

Trina was still polite. "Come on back, Felicia."

But I stopped Felicia with a wave of my hand. "I will allow her to do it this time, but next time you need to have an appointment." Stepping to the side, I let her pass. Even though Felicia had a slight smile plastered on her face, I could feel her eyes burning a hole through me. She wanted to curse me out but that bitch knew better. When they were out of the reception area I turned to Rochelle and at the same time we both mouthed, "Bitch." We laughed out loud.

Before long, my entire plans for the day had been changed. Hood called me up and told me that instead of meeting at the Outback Steakhouse later that evening he wanted me to go out that night and celebrate in honor of Rob. Initially they had planned to do it the week before I was in New York. But some of the crew had a change of plans. After leaving the salon I headed home for a bubble bath, some wine, and then some relaxation, and in that order, before getting dressed for the celebration at the club.

VIP was on fire from the time I stepped inside. The drinks were flowing, the DJ was on fire, and out of the speakers blared T.I. and Trey Songz's "2 Reasons." Hood hit the door taking shots of Don Julio. He was ready to celebrate to the fullest for Rob. The room was set up with plenty of memories of Rob. The big television screen on the wall was showing pictures of Rob from past gatherings with the crew and his family. Rob's baby momma, Leslie, had decided not to come. She was still in the grieving mode. The party was emotional but krunk at the same time. Rochelle had arrived before me and already had a drink in her hand. She pulled me away from Hood and handed me a shot of Patrón, which I gladly downed. Thinking about the earlier portion of the day, from Hood about to kill Silk to Felicia popping up at my salon, my day had been a little wild. I needed to have a good time.

An hour into the celebration, Silk arrived with Felicia proudly jumping off his arms.

"Don't tell me we got to party and drink with this hoe, too," Rochelle mouthed. Rochelle was full of Patrón and a shot or two of that Don Julio so one could only pray she behaved.

"I know, right." I laughed.

Before we knew it, Felicia had gotten a drink and made her way over to us. She stopped directly in front of me. Raising my glass to my lips, I took a drink and swallowed. Because the wrong word out of her mouth and her ass was mine. "Mya, I just wanted to tell you that Trina is a badass stylist. My shit is tight." She touched her hair in approval. Did she really believe she was telling me something that I didn't already know? Instead of replying with my voice, I gave her a tight-lipped smile. All her fakeness was getting on my nerves. I knew the bitch still held a grudge against me and Rochelle for beating her ass years ago. The neighborhood we grew up in, you didn't just forgive and forget.

I guess she realized I had no words for her, so she spoke up again. "Well, see you later, and I will be returning as a regular customer." She looked at Rochelle and smirked. Rochelle went to get in her face, but I blocked her path.

"Just make sure you have an appointment first," I replied. Without acknowledging what I said, she turned and strutted toward Silk. I knew she was trying to blow me off but she did not want to try me. Rochelle was shaking her head watching Felicia walk off.

"Mya, that bitch is bold. I told you she thinks that she is hot shit now, but she do one more cocky thing and I swear I'ma beat that ass." Rochelle rolled her eyes in Felicia's direction. "Bitch," she released, then polished off her drink.

I felt the same way. I knew Felicia was just trying to rub her newfound success with dating a baller in our face. For the rest of the night she was all over Silk, but a few times I felt him gawking in my direction. Each time I would almost catch him, he would try to play it off. But his wandering eye was getting on my last damn nerve.

After a while, Rochelle forgot all about Felicia and put her attention on Dontae. They danced and blazed together all night. I spent a lot of time thinking about Li'l Bo. I missed him so much. The celebration for Rob just made me realize my sufferings for my brother. Even though he had been gone for two years, it still felt fresh. Then Trey Songz's "Fumble" started banging out the speakers and Hood pulled me to the floor. As soon as we wrapped our arms around each other, his cell started to ring and vibrate. Instead of answering it, he wrapped me tighter in his arms, ignoring the ring. It stopped, but it quickly started up again. The song was about over and his phone was still ringing. Annoyed, I stopped and told him to answer it.

Hood glanced at the phone caller ID, then hit talk on the screen. "What, nigga?" he yelled into the phone over the music. The look on Hood's face immediately showed a sign of trouble. "Lock that shit down, shit better be tight when I get there. Buzz them other niggas off the block. Now," Hood yelled and ended the call.

"What happened, babe?" I asked as soon as he hung up.

"I gotta bounce. Have Rochelle drop you by the crib. A'ight."

"Babe, is everything okay?" I was worried. Calls like these meant trouble and the end of somebody's life.

"Later, a'ight." I knew that he would talk with me later; now was not the time. He leaned down and kissed me, then signaled Dontae, Rico, Pablo, and Silk, and they were out.

Rochelle rushed over to me. "What's going on, Mya?" Clueless, all I could do was shrug my shoulders.

"Just take me home." The night was over for me. It was a wrap.

Chapter 14

Turning over in bed, I peeked my head from under the covers and realized it was daylight. I reached over to the left of me and spread my fingers wide. Feeling an empty spot made it clear that Hood was not home yet. I grabbed my cell phone to check for missed calls. There were none. I also noticed that it was damn near noon and that made my heart drop. Sitting up in the bed, I slid my feet into my slippers just as Hood walked into our bedroom. Distress was all over his face. The look was familiar.

He dropped his keys on the bed, took both his hands and rubbed his face as a sigh escaped his lips. Anger was dripping from his veins and stinging at his bloodshot red eyes.

"What happened?" I prepared for the bad news.

"My trap spot over by the Brewster was jacked," he released with a sigh.

"They get away with the work?"

Hood looked at me and I knew that there was more that he was not telling me.

"What else, Hood? Tell me." I wanted to know. I braced myself for what he would say.

"Chuck bucked one of the niggas that jacked the spot. It was Anthony. That li'l nigga dead." For a minute I thought I heard him wrong. I asked him to repeat it.

"Chuck killed Anthony, the dude Monica messin' off wit'. Clearly them niggas don't know who they messin' wit'. I caught up to the other two, now they bodied. Sucka mothafuckas act like they know what time it is," Hood barked, moving on from the fact that Monica's new boyfriend was shot dead in his trap house.

I bit my bottom lip with confirmation. I knew that Anthony's ass was no good. And he had to be stupid, trying to jack one of Hood's spots. Clearly he had no idea who he was messing with. But forget him. I shook my head, feeling confused, because my next thought was Monica. She would know by now or would be finding out soon. She would be upset and I had to be there for her. I got up and started to get dressed. I had to get over to their crib.

Hood continued to ramble obscenities about fucking up this or that, but I heard nothing he said clearly. Finally, one of his questions got through. "Where are you going?"

"To check on Monica." I slid into a pair of pink-and-black Flight Jordan hightops. "I'll hit you later." I had gotten dressed in record time. Grabbing my cell off the nightstand, I all but dashed out of the room without so much as a good-bye to Hood. Besides, I knew he had business to tend to. I was sure he had only stopped by the crib to shower and hit the stone again.

"Yeah, check on her and make sure she's straight." By the time he said it, I had already made it to the stairs. I was in a hurry.

Using my key for the first time in a long time, I opened the door to find Ma coming out of the kitchen. The look on her face showed that she was not shocked to see me. My mother knew that regardless of any issue that Monica and I had, I would be there for her. I was consistent when it came to that.

"She's in the living room," she informed me without me saying another word.

With a couple of steps I was standing in the living room watching Monica. She sat on the couch as the television played. But I knew she wasn't watching it. Looking up at me, she gave me a quick glance and turned her attention back to the TV. Standing in one spot, I just watched her. Gradually the tears started to pour down her face. I walked over to the sofa and sat down next to her.

"I just found out..." Her voice was shaky. She wiped her tearstained face with her hand. Ma came out of the kitchen and handed her some Kleenex. Monica dabbed at tears that continued to flow one after the other. "I should have listened to you...I knew you were right about him."

I felt so bad, even though I knew what she said was true. But now was not the time for me to say *I told you so.* "It's not about that. I'm here for you." I reached out and hugged her. We held each other tight as she cried.

"I thought he would be different, Mya. I really did. But nope, just another two-bit stick-up man. It's either that or trapping." Monica broke our embrace as if something had just occurred to her.

"I bet Hood's pissed?" She searched my face for confirmation.

Smiling at her, I confirmed. "You know he is, but don't you worry about that. Anthony's fuck-up has nothing to do with you." I chuckled, hoping to cheer Monica up just a little. But no smile graced her face; instead another single teardrop formed in the crease of her eye socket.

"I just can't believe he would do that. He had to know that was Hood's spot. He should have known better."

"Look, you can't worry about that. It's done now. So do your best to forget about it."

"But will it always be like this? Am I ever going to meet some-one that is normal? I mean, will I ever find someone like Hood? He is an all-around good guy. Or will I only ever attract thugs with no future? Is it me, Mya?" Hearing her say this and question herself broke my heart. How could I reassure her that one day she would find the one? Hell, truth be told, Detroit was full of snakes. Losers looking for a quick and easy come-up. Either that or they were a monster waiting to beat the life out of you. But she was right: Even though Hood was in the game, he was a good guy. Somehow I had gotten lucky.

"Monica, you are only seventeen. You have forever to find the right guy. It is only natural at your age to attract thugs. Comes with the territory, but yes, you will find the right one. Just give yourself time. See, you are actually lucky. You gettin' all your experience while you are young. Five years from now you'll be a pro at dodging the losers. Trust me. You got this." I nudged her shoulder and smiled. And then finally, she smiled back at me. She trusted my judgment. I would never give her bad advice.

"I guess I believe you, you are normally right. I'm lucky to have a big sis like you." Monica reached over and tightly wrapped her arms around me. Now that caused tears to spill all over my face. We were such crybabies. I saw my ma watching us with a smile. She was proud we were always there for each other in our time of need. That was important for any family.

Monica wanted me to stay and hang out with them so I stayed over for a while. We ordered Chinese food and watched *Dreamgirls*. We both loved that movie. Monica seemed to have cheered up, but I knew she was having a hard time with her newfound situation. She had experienced death too much to be a fresh seventeen years old. I wanted so much more for her. I wanted her to have all that I did not have. And education was at the top of the growing list that I had generated for her. But I also knew that in life you needed more than books and degrees. Achievement was good, but happiness was very important also.

Chapter 15

Weeks had gone by since Anthony had been shot and killed in the process of jacking one of Hood's trap spots. Besides the fact that some of the dudes that had been involved had been dealt with, aka bodied, I knew nothing. Hood never really discussed the details of his dope business with me. I guess he figured the less I knew about his operation or empire, whatever he wanted to call it, the better it was for me. Not that I really cared. My only concern was him letting that life go. That was best for us as a family.

I had been spending as much time as I could free up with Monica. I wanted her to know that I was there to support her one hundred percent. Soon she would be done with high school and starting college. I wanted her to focus her energy on keeping her GPA up and taking care of Imani. To ease our minds, we had gone shopping and blew ten thousand easy. We spent that money on clothes, shoes, and whatever else her little heart desired while we were out. We loved to shop. For us it was a pressure release. My mom, on the other hand, threw her hands up at us and waved us off, telling us just pick her something up, because one thing she refused to do was go shopping with the two of us. According to her, we took absolutely too long when we shopped. But we had just been hanging out. I wanted to help Monica to keep her mind off Anthony and that entire situation as much as possible if I could.

Of course Monica assured me that she was okay or "over it," as she put it. But I knew that deep down she was hurting. She had decided it was best for her not to attend Anthony's funeral services. According to her, she was done with that situation and of course I was more than fine with that. He had crossed the line and unfortunately he paid a high price.

I had not been at the salon for three days because I had to be with my Monica. She needed her big sister around for moral support. So today I had gotten up bright and early, made breakfast for Hood, and broke out. I had two heads to do first thing in the morning. I was done before lunch. Hood had stopped by the salon to bring Rochelle and me a catfish plate. So we were just sitting around eating and chopping it up.

"So how Monica doin'? She over that bullshit with Anthony's punk ass?" Rochelle forked some coleslaw.

I allowed my sweet tea to slide down my throat before responding. I loved some ice cold sweet tea. "She cool."

"Good 'cause the last thing she need to be doin' is trippin'. That nigga had that comin'. Stick-up kids always pay the price. He should have known better." Rochelle may have seemed heartless, but like I always say, she keeps it one hundred.

"Yeah, I know. I'm just tryna keep her encouraged. She think that it's her own fault that she keep ending up with guys like that. Like she a curse or something."

"Ha, if that is the case, then I got it, too. Check my track record, let me see . . . Mike, the only good thing I got out of that was Tiny." Rochelle smiled. "Then Li'l Lo snuffed out by the game. And let's just be honest, Dontae ain't Carlton off the *Fresh Prince of Bel-Air.*" She chuckled. "If I ain't considered cursed with all that bad luck, then she good."

"Yeah, well, I have warned you about that Dontae. But you forgot about Todd. He is different from all of them other guys, he is a schoolteacher. Legal money." I laugh. "And you dumped him for it." I playfully shook my head.

Rochelle shut the lid on her fish plate. "Mya, now you lyin'. I did not dump him for that." She pointed her index finger at me and laughed.

"Then why? You still ain't never gave me a good reason." I popped my mouth from the good taste of that Frank's Red Hot sauce on my fish.

"Yes, I did. I told you he be damn serious all the time. I tried to tell him to chill wit' that. He ain't listen to me. That's his fault."

"Just like I thought. You like them thugs, Rochelle." I decided to keep it real.

Rochelle rolled her tongue around in her mouth like something was stuck in her back tooth. Then she smiled. "You right." We both giggled. Trina walked in staring at us.

"Okay, let me in on the joke. What's so damn funny? And you bitches ain't have to tell nobody y'all was getting fish." Trina pouted.

"Nothin', I'm just trippin' off ya girl here, Rochelle. She stay buckin' the system." Rochelle and I continued to laugh.

"Yeah and what about the fish?" Trina squinted her eyes at the both of us in accusation. "Y'all coulda told me. Now I gotta go pick up some." She pouted.

"Girl, Hood brought this fish over. Stop hatin'." Rochelle grinned.

"Hmmm." Trina twisted up her lips. "Well, y'all ready for this weekend? New York, hair show, party . . . all that." Trina checked her hair out in the mirror. Rochelle had hooked her up earlier with a twenty-piece quick weave with a highlight of orange and it was bangin'.

"You know it." Rochelle opened the lid back up on her plate and bit off her last piece of fish. "I can't wait. I started packing a week ago." Rochelle had her hand in front of her mouth since she was talking with a mouth full of food.

Trina looked at me through the mirror. "What about you, Mya? You don't seem amped about the trip. I already know you and Hood gone paint the town after we win all them awards and that cash," she chimed, still checking out her quick weave. No one could tell her that her hair was not the bomb 'cause she knew better.

"You already know. Shit, I'm ready. I just know that competition gone be tight this year. Mississippi gone be in the building, you know them bitches be doing hair in the kitchen. They shit be on point." I had to keep it real. Mississippi hairstylists brought it when they showed up. We were going to have to be on our hair game for real.

"Aww, don't worry 'bout that, we got this. Those bitches may do hair in the kitchen but we grew up dodging bullets doing hair outside in the ghetto. Trust me when I say we got this," Rochelle barked and she was serious. Her confidence not jaded.

"Rochelle, yo ass is crazy." I laughed. I really was not that nervous, but I did have mad respect for them Mississippi chicks 'cause they always brought their A game. But I was ready. I had tried to convince Monica to go. But she said she had a lot of studying to do since she had some major tests coming up. School was a top priority for her, but I knew Hood and Rochelle would be by my side so I was good.

Chapter 16

The day for us to leave for New York had finally arrived. My flight was due to leave in four hours and I was just packing. Normally, I would have been packed at least two days before, but shit had been crazy. I spent most of the day and part of the night at the salon with Rochelle, Trina, and Pam trying to get all the supplies we would be using ready to go. Some we had shipped overnight FedEx, the rest we would be taking with us on the plane. Then the models that I had chosen to be in the hair show had their flights canceled at the last minute. I had to get them rebooked and off because they were scheduled to have runway practice yesterday. If all that wasn't enough, when I finally drug my overexhausted body home, Hood hit me with the bad news that he could not go because he had unexpected business to tend to in Detroit. That pissed me all the way off. I was sick of the game interfering with our life, our plans. Most of all, I was tired of him allowing it.

So here I was, upset, trying to pack so that I would not miss my flight. Rochelle had called and said that she was about to leave her crib because she had to stop and pick up Trina. I knew I needed to put some pep in my step, but my heart was not in it. I was all but throwing my clothes into the Louis Vuitton suitcase that I was packing. Then I felt Hood walk up behind me and attempt to wrap his arms around my waist. This was the wrong move because I was not in the mood.

With slight force I unwrapped his arms from my waist. I didn't use excessive force, but I wanted him to know that I was serious. Now was not the time. I had been trying hard all day to control my anger. I just wanted to pack my stuff and get away for a while.

"What? Why you trippin', Mya?" Did he really have to ask that question? Had I been talking to a brick wall? I breathed in deep and bit my tongue.

I stopped packing for a second, then looked up at the wall without saying anything. Then I focused my attention back on the packing.

"So you just gone ignore me? You mad, right? You know I would go if I could." Why wouldn't he just shut up?

Damn, he was beginning to nag me. His babbling was going in one ear and seeping out of the other. I wanted him to drop it, but since he refused, I guessed he wanted to see the back side of my temper.

I turned around slowly and met him face to face since he was intent on being in my space. "I am so fuckin' sick of you with this dope game shit," I spat. "You give it ninety percent and me ten. You ain't going to New York so fuckin' what. I could care less about that because that is short term. No, this shit gets deeper than that. But you already made your choice. So please just get outa here so I can finish packin'!" I scream and turn back to my mission.

"Babe, this shit is for our future, can't you see?" He just would not stop trying to convince me.

I chuckled. He still didn't get it. "I am so damn . . . sick of you saying that," I seethed.

"I told you this job is important. I can't just walk away. You know that though. So why you trippin'? You already know what I gotta do."

My cell beeped, signaling a text. Then I remembered again that I had a plane to catch. "Hood, I have been warning you. Now you need to get it together. I won't keep repeating myself." I sighed then turned back to my suitcase. I felt like I was beating a dead horse. But I struck a button with my last statement.

"What do you mean you warned me? What you sayin'?" I had his attention. Now was the time for me to lay it on the line. I had tried talking to my husband. I had tried to reason with him. I had tried hard to get him to see why he should let the game go. But I could no longer sugarcoat the situation.

I slammed my Louis Vuitton suitcase closed. "If you don't leave the game alone, it's over between us. I will leave you. I would rather do that than sit around here and wait for someone to call me up to tell me you are dead or locked away for the rest of your life." I spoke without ever turning around to face him. My eyes were swollen with tears. I had finally said it.

"That's it," Hood yelled, standing behind me. "You just gone walk away from me like that? I'm your husband, Mya. Not your damn boyfriend. We have a commitment." I could hear the tears in his voice. My straightforward words had cut him deep. He had never considered that consequence.

"Yes, we have a commitment, but you don't stand behind it. You jeopardize it. And I won't live like that." Tears ran down my face rapidly. Hood started to wrap his arms around me again. This time I moved out of his embrace. I could not give in. He had to get it together or else I was done.

"Mya, Mya." He stood behind me chanting my name, but I was done responding. There was nothing else I could say. I had said everything that was relevant to me.

"You know what? You trippin'." His voice was full of anger as he turned and left the room. I felt emptiness where his presence had been. I was done. After I finished packing, I grabbed my bags and took them to the car. I had to hurry up so that I would not miss my flight. At this very moment Hood and I were officially in a bad place in our relationship. I had never imagined that we could be here.

Chapter 17

The Detroit Metro Airport was busy for a Sunday. Rochelle, Trina, and I had just touched back down from New York. After grabbing our luggage, we headed outside to the parking lot to catch a shuttle back to our vehicles. Hood had offered to drop me off at the airport a thousand times before he finally got the picture that I was not having it.

Even though I had left home pissed off as FUCK, the trip to New York turned out great. My girls and I turned up. We painted New York red for three days and two nights. We won first place in the hair show, bringing in fifty thousand dollars! As the girls and I said our good-byes, my cell started to ring. I knew who it was without looking at the screen. It was singing Tamar's "Love and War," the ringtone that I set up for Hood. I quickly pushed ignore and started up the ignition on the Escalade. I had ignored his calls the whole time I was in New York. Once I touched down in New York, I texted him letting him know that I had made it safely. After all, I didn't want him to worry, but I didn't have anything to say to him.

As soon as I walked into the house, the aroma of food cooking hit me and tortured my nostrils. It smelled like one of my favorites: spicy orange chicken stir-fry. I loved it. But I was not hungry. I had eaten a full meal before getting on the plane. The girls and I had partied so much the night before, we had to eat something to energize ourselves and to dry up the Patrón from the previous night.

Hood stepped into the foyer and greeted me. "So I see you made it safely."

Without an answer I stepped around him and headed toward the kitchen. "Damn, it's like that? I don't get a hello or hug? Shit, you have already ignored all my calls since you been gone. A nigga must be on permanent punishment."

"Hi, Hood." I turned around and spoke with sarcasm in my voice.

"That was a'ight, but a hug would be better." He smiled and came closer to me, wrapping his arms around me, and hugged me tight. I accepted the hug, but my stubbornness refused to allow me to hug him back. Releasing myself from his embrace, I turned to continue toward the kitchen.

"I figured you would be hungry so I had Harold the Chef come in and do your favorite orange chicken stir-fry." I was sure this was part of his peace offering.

Opening up the fridge, I grabbed a Diet Pepsi and turned to leave the kitchen. When I turned around, Hood was standing behind me. The look on his face was so sincere. He could not take me being mad at him. I almost caved in. The sight of him made me weak. I loved him that much. But he left me no choice. "I'm not hungry. I ate before getting on the plane." I stepped around him and headed for the stairs.

Not willing to give up, he followed. "Well, maybe we can watch a movie. I'm in for the night. I left Pablo in charge."

"Not tonight, Hood. I'm tired. All I want to do is take a shower and climb into bed and sleep."

After my shower, I called Monica to see what they had been up to while I was away. We chopped it for a minute. I started to yawn, so I told her good-bye then I pulled the covers back on the bed and slid in. My body screamed out from the comfort. I had been waiting three days to get back to my bed. Within seconds I felt sleep taking over. I felt like I was wrapped in a cloud. Sleep had claimed me, but I stirred as I felt Hood's strong arms wrapping around me and then his soft lips caressing my neck. My middle screamed to be with him but again my stubbornness disapproved.

Slightly facing him, I responded, "I'm tired." I turned my back to him and snuggled closer into my pillow and wrapped my sheet around me extra tight.

"A'ight. Get your rest." Sliding closer to me, he softly kissed my left shoulder before I felt him turn over on his side of the bed. That was the first time I had ever denied him. He didn't argue with me about it. Hood was always a gentleman when it came to me. He always let me have my way. Nevertheless, if he did not get his act together, it damn sure wouldn't be the last time I denied him. As much as I loved him, I meant it when I said I would leave him.

I was up bright and early to head to the bank and then the shop. Rochelle had already called my house phone to let me know that Kelly, one of my clients, had called looking for me. When I had hung up after talking to Monica the night before, I powered my phone off. I wanted to sleep eight hours with no interruptions. So I know Kelly was in a panic. She worked for a law firm and she wanted every string on her head in place. Apparently she had partied all weekend and now her head was in need of my touch. Lucky for her, I had no one scheduled, so I told Rochelle to have her meet at nine a.m.

Before I went to the salon, I had to run by the bank to deposit the fifty-thousand-dollar check we won in New York. I had to put it into my business account so that I could pay the models who had performed on my company's behalf. Then I would take the rest and divide it up between Rochelle, Trina, Renee, and myself.

"Is she happy now?" Rochelle asked me as I approached the area in the salon where we took breaks from time to time.

"Girl, yes." Rochelle was eating some popcorn. I reached for her bag to grab a few, then sat down.

"Mya, she was on ten when she could not get you on the phone. Talk about panic. She was trippin'." Rochelle smiled as she described Kelly's behavior earlier. Sometimes Kelly could be a little dramatic, but she was a loyal client.

"I know, right. Girl Kelly's ass is a perfectionist. Plus she is trying to make partner so she be wanting every aspect of her life to be perfect. Except the fact she still be hittin' them blunts." I had to admit I had been shocked when she told me she got high. I would never have guessed it.

"Oh snap, she get down like that?" Rochelle seemed surprised. "She always seem uptight to me." Rochelle judged, but meant no harm.

"Hell yeah, she a weed head."

"Dang, I woulda never guessed that. But, girl, guess who shows up at my house last night unannounced?" I knew this would be good.

"Who? And please don't say Mike."

"Girl, boo, don't do me. He knows better. The only times he ever shows up is to pick up Tiny and we schedule a time for that." Rochelle popped her mouth and rolled her eyes. Mike would forever be on her shit list. "Anyways, it was Todd." She breathed hard.

"Oh, what he want?" I was surprised to hear that he had come by. She broke the poor dude's heart.

"Talkin' 'bout how much he miss me and Tiny. Sayin' we are a major part of his life and he can't just give us up." Rochelle's facial expression was sarcastic.

I smiled. "Awww, that is so sweet. What did you say, Rochelle?" The smile on my face quickly turned to suspicion. I knew she could be mean on purpose and poor Todd was bound to be her victim.

"Hmmph," Rochelle sighed, rolling her eyes. "I told him the truth, that I was seeing someone," she stated simply.

"Rochelle, why you tell that dude that . . . especially after he done poured his heart out to you. You so damn mean," I scold her.

"What you expect me to do, lie to him?" Rochelle crossed her arms and seemed to soften. "But I did kinda feel bad, though. He was hurt. It was written all over his face. But I just didn't know what else to do." She sighed. "Besides, it's his own fault for showing up without calling first. I mean who does that?" Rochelle looked at me like she was looking for me to answer her. That chick is funny.

"Shit, it's on him." Rochelle had turned from being sympathetic back to her stubborn self.

"Ummm." I started shaking my head. "You will never learn."

"I guess not. But I sure did not want him to leave afterwards. I wanted to ask him if he would hit it. Girl, Todd is the shit in bed." I could not believe her nerve. My mouth flew open from shock. She had a lot of audacity.

"What?" I started laughing. There was no changing Rochelle. "You are so crazy! How you gone break dude's heart then ask him to jump yo bones, Rochelle?" I could not stop laughing at her, she was a mess. We both laughed for a minute. As my smile faded, I started to think about Hood and our relationship. I had no idea that Rochelle was watching me.

"Enough about me." Rochelle's smile had faded. "What's up with you? When you gone tell me? And don't try to say nothing, I know you, Mya. Something is bothering you. I could see it even while we were in New York. Yeah, you turned up, but I could still tell something was eating at you. Now go ahead and spit it out."

She was right. I knew she could read me the same way I could tell when something was not right with her. But I hated to stress her with my problems. She had her own emotions she was still working through. But I guess that's what friends are for. Even still, my words would not come. I just wanted to swallow my pain and move on to what was next.

"Is it Hood?" she finally asked me directly.

As soon as his name came out of her mouth my heart dropped. My feelings went to my shoulders. Without answering, I nodded my head yes. Rochelle quickly got up and came to me. Bending down, she embraced me.

"Don't cry, Mya. You know I'm here for you. Why you ain't tell me? What that nigga do?" Rochelle broke our embrace and looked at me as if she was ready to go kick Hood's ass.

I had to laugh at her 'cause I knew she was serious. "Girl, why you always ready to fight," I sniffed.

"You know how I gets down." She smiled back.

I sniffled again and wiped at my tears with my bare hand. Rochelle grabbed a napkin off the table and handed it to me. "It's the game, this dealing and all that. I just can't do this shit no more." Tears poured down my face. "I have had enough of that life."

"I understand how you feel, Mya. But that's what he do. How you just gone ask him to give that up? Just like that, walk away. That's his bread and butter." She kicked it to me straight and I knew Rochelle was just being realistic.

"You sound just like him." I chuckled and sniffed at the same time. "So you also know just like him that we don't need the money. We got plenty." Rochelle shook her head in agreement.

"But it doesn't matter the reason anymore. I feel strongly about it and I gave him an ultimatum. It has to be me or the game." I was matter-of-fact. "One or the other, he can't have them both."

"What does he think about all this?" she asked.

"He says he hears me, but that's about it. Now, when I said I would leave him, that pissed him off. But other than that, I don't know. I haven't been talkin' to him. I been playing the silent treatment card. He suffering from it, too."

"Oh and you accuse me of being mean." We both chuckled.

"I know, right. I just don't know what else to say, Rochelle. I just know I can't lose him to these streets. I mean, look around: Li'l Bo, Pig, Li'l Lo . . . and don't forget Rob, all dead. And for what? I cannot lose . . . NO, I won't lose him to that." I stressed that part, meaning every word. I would fight for my man's life or walk away from it.

"Damn, Mya, I never looked at it like that." Rochelle had begun to tear up, but she grinned. "Yo ass is a poet."

Now she was forcing it. "Get outa here." I threw my wet napkin at her and we both started laughing. All of a sudden we hear what appears to be yelling.

"That's Pam. Who is she arguing with?" Rochelle looked at me. We both jumped up and ran toward the reception area. We slowed down as we entered to find Pam holding her own as Felicia, along with two other chicks standing behind her, continued to yell something about bullshit.

Instead of addressing Felicia's ratchet behavior, I looked to Pam for answers. "Pam, what is going on?" I pretended as if Felicia was not standing there.

"Well, she upset..." Before Pam could finish, Felicia jumped in.

"Why you askin' her? Ask me, I'm the customer. Besides, it should be clear what my problem is, look at my head." She pointed at her hair and it was a mess, just like her attitude. "I need to see Trina." She twisted her lips and threw her left hand on her hip while balancing her Gucci bag with her right arm.

I slowly turned in Felicia's direction and prayed silently to keep my cool. The last thing I wanted was to start a fight in my salon. After all, it was a business. But by then Rochelle had had it.

"Bitch, who do you think..." Rochelle jumped in Felicia's face, but Pam and I pulled her back in time.

"Chill, Rochelle, I will handle this." I tried to control the situation and keep Rochelle off Felicia's ass.

Rochelle sighed and mouthed to me, "You better get her."

As calmly as I could muster, I turned back to face Felicia. "Felicia, do you have an appointment?"

"Hell no," she barked at me with attitude.

At that point my patience was thin. Clearly this bitch didn't respect my place of business. But with a tight lip, I gave it another try. "Felicia, this is a business. I'ma need you to fall back and respect my customers. If you can't do that, then hit the pavement." I was proud of myself: In the past my hands would have been around her chicken-thick neck. "Besides, Trina is not here yet." I smirked.

"Look, Mya, I need to get my hair done. Ain't you got somebody else up here that can do me?" She just would not let up.

"No, Felicia. I don't have people sitting around waiting for walk-ins. This is an upscale salon, we do heads by appointment only. We have a full clientele. But I would be more than willing to allow Pam to schedule you an appointment." Again I smirked. I was loving the pissed-off look on her face. Standing beside me, Rochelle had a grin on her face.

I turned to Pam and told her to set her up with the next available appointment spot that Trina had open. With that said, I turned and headed toward the back, but Felicia was not done.

"All you bitches just jealous of me." Felicia chuckled from deep in her throat. "Mya, fuck you and this raggedy-ass salon. Ugh, wit' yo wannabe perfect ass, but I know about what you did to Squeeze's operation." I felt the color drain from my face. How did she know about that? I guess I didn't kill Charlene's big mouth ass fast enough before she got a chance to run it. Her next obscenity snatched my thoughts back. "Bitch!!"

At that point I was done. That bitch had tried it. This was a check her ass was gonna have to cash. Before I could stop or control myself, I turned around and rushed her. My right fist connected with her left eye socket and she screamed out. But that didn't last long because next I wrapped my hands around her neck. Then I threw her to the floor and punched her over and over until Rochelle, Pam, and two clients pulled me off her.

"You dumb bitch! Come up in my salon startin' shit. I'll choke your ass to sleep," I yelled, meaning every word. I had tried hard to be professional, but no, this bitch just wanted to disrespect me. I was heated.

The girls who were with her, aka her bodyguards, just stood back and watched as Felicia attempted to get up. Rochelle pulled back deep in her throat and hocked spit on her then yelled, "Bitch! And don't come back. 'Cause next time I'ma beat that ass," she threatened.

Felicia got up with tears running down her face. "Fuck you back, bitch!" She cried and screamed at the same time. "This ain't over. I will have the last laugh," she screamed out before Pam and one of our clients, Tunya, pushed her out the door. That whole incident was crazy. I could not believe Felicia. She had some nerve. She had come looking for trouble and she found it.

Chapter 18

I still could not believe Felicia had come to my salon and showed out the way she did. Two days had gone by and I was still in awe of the nerve of that hoe. Not to mention she tried to bring up the issue with Squeeze. She had known about the robberies all along and I knew exactly where she got the information: Charlene. But I just brushed it off, though. That was in the past and, besides, Squeeze was dead now. And really, what's a dead drug dealer to do? Fuck Squeeze and her. I just hate that she had to bring it up. Rochelle had not brought it up or asked me anything, but the curious look on her face was enough. She wondered what Felicia was talking about.

I called Hood right after and told him what had happened. Hood's exact words were "Fuck that bitch. She disrespects, she can get it." I assured him that the bitch got it. She knew better than to act a fool with me. I guess the last ass whupping Rochelle put on her wasn't enough. At the same time I didn't want to cause conflict with Silk and Hood, because niggas sometimes go wacko over their females. Hood happened to be that dude. Not that I cared about the deal they had going on. 'Cause I could care less about that. It's just that when dudes start beefing instead of fighting, there's bloodshed. And to be honest, it was not that deep. Felicia just wanted to show her ass to get some attention. But Hood had assured me that everything was cool and for me to keep it moving 'cause, "Silk didn't want none. He should teach his bitch to behave." He even said that he was going to let Silk know that he didn't appreciate Felicia coming to my place of business and acting up.

Today the salon was closed, which meant Rochelle and I had the day off. Tiny was with Mike for the week so Rochelle said she would come by. We both had been so tired from working that we decided to watch a movie instead of going out shopping. *Kill Bill* was one of our favorites, so that was the choice. After that, we were going to watch *Alex Cross* with Tyler Perry. Both movies were packed with action. I could not wait. It had been a minute since we had movie day at my crib. I had a home theater built into my house with a huge-ass movie screen with all the trimmings, surround sound and all. We had the movie theater seats installed and a built-in popcorn machine, too. We hardly ever used that, though, I would just throw a bag of popcorn in the microwave.

I got up and made Hood breakfast early in the morning and now lunch was approaching. Rochelle had agreed to stop by Domino's and pick up a couple of pizzas for the movie. Hood was lying around the house, too; he had a meeting in a couple of hours, so while he waited he decided to watch *The Sopranos*. That was one of his favorite television shows. He loved to watch those reruns. He swore that they were going to bring that show back. But I knew better, so I just laughed at him and told him he had a better chance of *The Wire* coming back on television.

The doorbell rang twice so I knew Rochelle had finally arrived. I was in the kitchen grabbing paper plates for the pizza. We also had snacks like popcorn, Nerds, and oatmeal pies. You name it, we had it. It was going down. Hood answered the door. I could hear him and Rochelle talking, heading toward the kitchen.

"What's up, chick? 'Bout time you made it. Yo ass ain't never on time," I joked.

"Ha, ha, whatever." Rochelle sat the pizzas down on the table. "Even when I'm late I be on time. And I know you ain't watchin' nobody time. Don't make me bust on you." Rochelle tried to hoe me. We laughed. Hood just shook his head at both of us.

"How about both of y'all be late," Hood threw in. Turning to face him at the same time, we gave him the evil eye with the raised eyebrow. That meant his ass had tried it. He quickly caught the hint.

"A'ight, I'm gone. Just let me grab some of the pizza. Rochelle, I know you got some supreme up in here." That was his favorite and he made sure everyone knew it.

"Dude, I got you. Third box," Rochelle confirmed as she lifted the lid on the supreme. The steam off the pizza escaped the box. Damn, it looked good.

"What about the pepperoni?" I butted in. Now that was my favorite and Rochelle knew better than to come over without it. She didn't even answer me. She just raised the lid of the box next to the supreme and gave me a smile.

"Now that's what's up." I grinned, rubbing my hands together symbolizing it's on. "All right, let's grab some slices so we can get to the movie. Babe, you already got the screen going, right?" I always had Hood go and start the projector. There were too many buttons, so I hated operating it.

"Yep, it's ready to go." After piling pizza on a couple of paper plates, we headed to the theater room. The movie was already rolling through previews. I loved the loud booms that came from the surround sound. It always gave me that rush and got me pumped for the movie even if I had seen it a dozen times. Rochelle and I chose to sit in the back row. Before the movie could even get started good, I was on my second slice of pepperoni. Dang, it was banging.

The movie was banging as well. We were on a scene where Uma Thurman was fighting the chick with the patch on her eye in the trailer. That was one of my favorite parts. Uma was kicking that bitch's ass off top. But the hoe just kept coming back, sort of like Felicia. Rochelle and I cracked up as Uma reached her hands out and pulled that chick's other eyeball out of the socket. That shit was disgusting. Rochelle screamed out and shuddered as Uma held the eyeball.

"That is so disgusting, but she a bad bitch."

"I know, right." I laughed and popped some popcorn in my mouth.

"But I ain't gone lie, that look like you beating Felicia's ass the other day." Rochelle laughed and I chimed in. Her ass was crazy. I had to admit I went ham, but that's what I do. Never push me to that limit. I tried to let the bitch walk away several times but she just refused to walk away. In the end her mouth got the best of her and I got in that ass. And leave it up to Rochelle to compare it to Uma Thurman kicking ass on *Kill Bill*. The more I thought about it, the harder I laughed, and so did Rochelle. Then I noticed that Rochelle stopped laughing and focused on me. I had to get the giggles under control.

"So for real, what was that shit about when Felicia tried to pop off something about Squeeze operation? Ain't that nigga like missing or some? Like what dealings you ever had wit' him?" And there it was. The question I knew was coming. The nerves in my stomach started to flutter so I took a huge swig of my Coke. Fuck Felicia and her big-ass mouth.

"Aww, that hoe ain't talkin' 'bout nothin'." I tried to laugh it off. "She just mad 'cause I beat that ass." I should have slapped myself. That statement was lame, even I knew it, but I had nothing else. I felt awful lying to Rochelle, and the look on her face told me that she was well aware that I was full of shit.

"Mya, how long we been friends? How long I been holding you down as a friend?" Turning her entire body to face me, Rochelle was reading all my expressions. I was trapped, so I decided to lay it on the line.

"Like forever. So long, hell, I don't even remember." She had me with that: I couldn't lie to her. I had to tell her something. I had dreaded this moment since those words had spilled out of Felicia's mouth. And to be honest, at this point I was trapped.

"If we been friends for so long and we been through thick and thin, why the secrets? You are keeping something from me and I know it. I know you, Mya, and you nervous right now. I blew up your spot."

"A'ight, there were some things that happened back a little over two years ago...." I paused and took another drink—my throat was hella dry. Rochelle's eyes were glued to me. And I'm sure she wanted to take my Coke and throw it at the movie screen so that I could get to the point.

"Okay, remember..." I paused again. I had to think of the best way to say this.

Rochelle was growing impatient. She shifted her weight in her seat, but still her eyes never left me. She sighed. "Dang, Mya, just spit it out."

I took a deep breath in and went in. "Back when Squeeze's crew was getting robbed, I was responsible. I'm the one that robbed Luscious and Phil. That's how I came up with all that money." The look on Rochelle's face was priceless: Her mouth literally hung open with her bottom lip damn near touching her chin. One thing was for certain, I had shocked the hell out of her. Finally her lips touched again.

"Wait, you mean the hundred thousand dollars that you said your dad's friend had for you was all a lie? You got that gwap from robbing Luscious's punk ass?"

"Exactly."

"You mean to tell me you robbed both them punk-ass niggas and they didn't know you was a female?"

"Nope. I had on a mask and I disguised my voice. They never knew." I too still had a hard time believing I had pulled that off all by myself.

"How...I mean why?" Rochelle still had questions.

"Squeeze's ass is the one that beat Ma. It was him who did that horrible shit to her. That pushed me over the edge, so I decided to get even with him. The one thing I knew would hurt him was someone taking his money. So I did it. To be honest, it turned out to be easier than I thought it would," I bragged. While I still hated Squeeze, I was not proud of what I had done. But I damn sure didn't regret it.

Rochelle seemed to be thinking over everything. I tried to read her expression, but it was hard. By this time she had dropped her head a little so I couldn't see her eyes anymore. Something told me that as a best friend she felt betrayed. We were supposed to tell each other everything, and for that I was sorry. But I had my reasons. I had to protect her. Sometimes knowing is not such a good thing. Sometimes it's what you don't know that keeps you safe from harm.

Rochelle raised her head and looked at me. "So basically you lied to me. Me, your best friend for over twelve years? And for what? You are supposed to be able to share everything with me."

"Rochelle, you right and that is true. But not this, this you were better off not knowing, so I made that decision." And that was real. I hope she would one day understand that.

"Mya, you went out and you robbed crew members of what was at that time one of the biggest dope pushers on the street. Do you know how funkin' dangerous that was? We was still hangin' as usual and you never once told me. How could you keep something like that from me?"

"Like I said, I had to. It was for the best. I never told a soul, not even Hood knows about this. You are the first." That was another lie. Hood did know, but not because I told him. Squeeze's punk ass had ratted me out on the night he kidnapped me. I could tell I still was not getting through to her. She felt betrayed.

"You know what? I'm out." Rochelle bent down and started to put her shoes back on. She was hurt. I had to fix this.

"But that's not all."

Rochelle looked up, rolled her eyes at me, and went back to putting on her shoes.

"I killed Phil," I released.

"You what?" Rochelle all but screamed.

"Shhh, I don't want Hood to hear." She got quiet instantly, but her eyes asked the burning question: What happened? But I decided to remain quiet to make her verbally ask me why.

"I had to. He tried to rape me." Again the look on Rochelle's face showed shock, but when I said the word *rape,* tears spilled from her eyes and stung at mine. I tried to fight it, but just thinking back at that whole incident was my soft spot. I still could remember the weight of Phil as I fought him off. I could still remember the sound of his body hitting the floor as I pushed him away. That dead weight was awful. And even though I had killed again since then, each killing carried its own weight. None was the same.

"Phil was my bait to robbing Squeeze. All the information I used to get the upper hand on robbing Squeeze's crew I got from Phil. Eventually Phil put two and two together and realized it was me who was pulling off the robberies. Long story short, he threatened to tell Squeeze if I didn't give him some of the money. But I knew his snake ass was just gone keep trying to play me for more money. So I snuck in his crib to talk to him on my terms so that we could work something legit out. That's when he beat me and tried to rape me. So I shot him."

Tears had been running down Rochelle's face, but suddenly a cry escaped. She reached out and hugged me. "Awww, Mya, I am so sorry you went through all that alone. I wish I could have been there for you. But I understand why you didn't tell me." I gave a sigh of relief. I was so happy she understood.

However, at the same time I still felt like shit because I decided not to share with her the story about Squeeze and Charlene's deaths. There was no way I could tell her I had killed them, too. She might start to think I'm a monster. Besides, she didn't need to know that. As far as she or anyone else knew, Charlene and Squeeze were two missing people. Who needed to know different? Everyone knew that snakes always got what they deserved: the bottom of the boot.

Later that day, after Rochelle left, Hood returned home and wanted to play a game of dominoes. He was winning his fifth game when I got a call from Trina. She wasn't feeling well and asked me to come by her house with a pregnancy test. According to her, she had been nauseated and she thought she might be pregnant. I was just glad to finally hear from her. She had not been to work in two days. She had called and left a message saying she would not be in for a couple of days. But after that we heard nothing else from her. Rochelle, Pam, and I had tried to reach her but only got her voicemail. I had even swung by her house the day before but got no answer. I was so worried I had made up my mind that if we didn't hear from her by the next day I would contact the cops. Trina didn't have any family in Detroit; they all lived in Alabama. So, basically, Rochelle and I were her family.

I told her to give me an hour or so and I would be by. I decided not to question her over the phone. After packing my mace in my Prada bag, I bounced out. I never knew if Teddy's punk ass wanted to start tripping. 'Cause that fool was buck wild. I stopped through Walgreen's and picked up an E.P.T. pregnancy test and headed over to Trina's crib.

I knocked at least six times before she finally opened the door. She looked like shit. She had on a pair of old red cut-up Levi's with a blue wifebeater and her hair was indescribable. It looked like half of her tracks were missing. Nothing on her was swollen, but to me she looked like she had had a fight and lost. I had never seen her look like this before, especially her clothes. I mean, I had seen her with black eyes, but not tore up from the floor up. But surprisingly, she wore a smile on her face. I on the other hand was horrified. This look had Teddy all over it.

I stood still at the door. I was in shock. I could not move. I just stared at her. "Mya, are you gone come in or what?" Trina held the door open with her left arm.

Without one word I reluctantly stepped into her apartment. I looked around and thought that everything seemed normal in the

apartment. It was immaculate, just as always. Nothing was out of
place. Then Teddy stepped around the corner. I wanted to spit on
him just because, but I chilled.

"Hey, what's up, Mya?" He spoke to me like we were friends. I
had to bite my lip to keep from cussing his ass out. I could not
stand him.

"Nothing," I answered dryly. Then I turned my attention back
to Trina. Who for odd reasons still wore that silly-ass smile. I rolled
my eyes at her.

"What the hell you smiling so hard for?" I asked.

"Dang, why you in a bad mood?" Trina slammed the door shut
and threw her right hand on her hip.

"Whatever, here." I handed her the Walgreen's bag.

"Good, you brought it. Thanks, Mya."

"You a'ight?" I asked.

"Yeah, I'm cool. Just been sick. Come on, let's go back to my
room." She turned and started toward the hall, but stopped to talk
with Teddy.

"Babe, you can go ahead and play your game. We gone be in
the back."

"A'ight," Teddy replied, then looked at me.

"Yo, Mya, when Hood gone hook me up?" I could not believe his
nerve. Whatever gave him the idea that Hood would fuck with him?

"Hook you up wit' what? Teddy, I don't know what you talkin' about. You need to holla at Hood."

"Awww, come on, Mya. Ask him when he gone put a nigga
on. Shidd, we gotta eat over this way, too. A nigga straight, but I
need to get my lady up out the hood. I wanna get her some of that
fine shit like you got. Feel me?" This dude was stupid for real.
What he needed to do if he wanted to help Trina was keep his
damn hands to himself. And what nigga told a female to ask her
man to hook him up? It was official in my book, Teddy was a low
life.

"Like I said, Teddy, holla at Hood." That was my final say on that. Now all I needed Teddy to do was exit stage left out of my damn face or his ass was gonna get maced. Trina saved him.

"Babe, stop badgering Mya. She came over to visit me." Trina smiled and reached up and kissed Teddy on the cheek.

"Oh, my bad, Mya. I ain't mean no harm. Y'all go ahead and do your thang." Trina turned to walk away and Teddy patted her on the ass. I almost threw up in my mouth. Like I said, I did not like him at all. I knew his affection could turn into a black eye or busted lip later.

Once we were inside Trina's room, she shut the door.

"I'm sorry about that, Mya. I don't know why Teddy insists on embarrassing himself. Him and his pipe dreams of being a big dope pusher get on my damn nerves. I keep tellin' him to just get a real job. But he won't listen." She hunched her shoulders.

"Girl, I ain't thinkin' about Teddy. I do wish he would not talk to me, though. He know I can't stand him."

"I know, right." Trina laughed. "But thank you so much for bringing this over. I just need to know. I have been feeling like crap, throwing up and not sleeping well."

"Well, just take the test. But what I really wanna know is why you ain't been to work in two days?"

"I told you I been feelin' bad."

"Then why can't you pick up the phone when we call? We all were blowing your phone up. I even came by yesterday and beat the door down. So where were you?"

"Oh, yesterday Teddy had to pick up Cynthia from Lansing for his mom. And I rode with him. We didn't get back until last night."

"Well, you should not worry people like that."

"I'm sorry," she apologized.

"You sure you are okay? How has Teddy been treating you?" I still was not convinced. I had to be sure.

"Teddy has been really sweet. We haven't been arguing or anything. These last couple of days we have been just spending quality time together. He is trying, Mya. We wanna get married and start a family one day." Now that statement shocked me. I think I blinked twice. The thought of her marrying that monster frightened me. I knew controlling woman beaters didn't change overnight, so I was sure Trina had been sipping on that stupid juice. Besides, had she looked in the mirror?

"Well, why do you look like this? Have you seen yourself? Because to be honest you look a hot mess." I had to keep it real with her. Clearly all the mirrors in the apartment were covered. And I knew she didn't go to Lansing looking like this. Something smelled fishy. But that smile was still planted on Trina's face. I wanted to smack it off.

"Oh, this mess." She looked down at her clothes then ran her fingers through her jacked-up weave . . . or what once had been her weave. I'm not sure how to describe it. She looked homeless for real. "Girl, I was so sick this morning I just threw this on. I had planned to do my own hair, but I started feeling so awful I just couldn't."

I pondered what she said and, to be honest, it did sound truthful. I guess being nauseated could change your appearance. Normally anything dealing with the stomach could throw anyone off their game. At that point I just decided to let it go. If she say she was happy, I had to believe her. Like the old saying goes, "If you like it, I love it."

"All right. But next time you off, just answer when your friends call. We worry about you and just want to be sure you are okay, okay?"

"Awww, look at you being all mushy." Trina reached over and hugged me. I laughed and hugged her back.

"Now get off me—you look diseased," I joked and playfully pushed her off.

We talked for another hour before Trina finally built up the nerve to take the test. Besides, I was getting tired. I had had a long day. Confessing to Rochelle took a lot of emotional strength. I had played and lost in dominoes with Hood. Then Trina dragged me out of the house to bring her the damn pregnancy test. It was late and I needed to get home and get some rest. The test revealed that Trina was not pregnant, which was shocking with all the symptoms she was having. But after Trina revealed that her and Teddy had eaten Coney dogs on the highway on their journey back from Lansing, we both chalked the throwing up to food poisoning or some twenty-four-hour bug. Satisfied with the conclusion and after rolling my eyes at Teddy, I jumped in my white Range Rover and balled out.

Chapter 19

"How are things at the salon?" Ma asked. We had been seated at a booth in the bar area at Red Lobster. Monica was taking a half day at school because she had an early appointment. So we decided that it would be a good day for the three of us to meet at one of our favorite eating spots.

"Everything's straight. Business is good as usual. Our clientele is on point. All of my stylists are booked with loyal clients. At this point it is really hard for new people to get their foot in the door," I was proud to say.

"That's what's up. I'm glad I got my spot secured," Monica said with a grin. She got top benefit being my sister. I kept her hair tight and she rocked all the newest styles that high school chicks craved.

"No doubt. You know you good. You my baby sis, I can't have you walking around with a nappy kitchen. Might ruin my own reputation, and I can't have that." We both grinned. "Speaking of which, Ma, when you gone let me get back in your kitchen? It's time for you to give that ponytail up," I joked, looking directly at Ma with a silly grin on my face. She had always been cautious about me getting in her head. Even now that I was licensed with my own shop, things had not changed. Marisa did not play when it came to her hair.

"For real, Mya, I am with you on that one. I get sick of that ponytail, too," Monica threw in. We both had tried everything to get her to change her mind. She needed a hair makeover as soon as possible, but convincing her to do it was like pulling teeth with a string: damn near impossible.

"Look, both of you can lay off my hairdo. I got this." She grabbed her ponytail and tossed it off her shoulder. After all these years, her hair still hung down her back. Normally she kept it across her neckline onto her shoulder. I had to admit, though, she rocked that ponytail. But it was just time for her to step it up. I could hook her up with that banger hairdo if she ever gave me the chance.

"Come on, Ma, dang, I have a license, for crying out loud. The state says I'm certified. You could trust me. I promise not to cut or burn too much off." I laughed, knowing she would not cave until she was ready. She could be stubborn like that sometimes.

"Oh hell, no. I don't like that sneaky look on your face. Forget it." We all cracked up. The waitress approached our table to take our order. We all ordered lobster tails, steamed broccoli, Caesar salads, and Pepsis to drink. The waitress grabbed up our menus and excused herself.

"But okay, I will think about it. I'll call you if I need an appointment. Sometimes I do get tired of washing all this." She playfully rubbed her ponytail. "A couple of months back I thought about calling up Suzie. Remember, she did it for years?" She shrugged, then got quiet as the waitress delivered the drinks, salads, and a basket full of garlic cheese biscuits. Each one of us followed the basket with lustful eyes. We loved those damn biscuits.

"Damn, that was quick." I watched the waitress as she walked away.

"I know, right," Monica agreed. "But, oh well, my stomach is growling." She reached for a biscuit and took a huge bite. Satisfaction was all over her face. Confirmation that the biscuit was the bomb.

For some reason, though, my mind wandered back to Ma's last statement about Suzie. She had been Ma's beautician for years before Dad had gone to prison. They were like friends. She went to Suzie every Friday, rain, sleet, or hailstorm, and Suzie kept her hair tight. I cannot recall one hairstyle that was not flawless. I had not thought about Suzie in years. But Ma bringing up her name suddenly made me think about her.

"So Ma, you say you almost called up Suzie. Why didn't you?" I forked some Caesar salad into my mouth. The dressing was bomb! I let the taste marinate on my tongue.

Chewing the biscuit that was in her mouth, Ma looked at me, then Monica, and then swallowed hard. I could tell she was pondering what she was about to say. Before speaking, she took a sip of her drink. At this point I forked another round of salad and Monica took a swig of her drink. Finally, Ma sighed. "Apparently, your dad and Suzie were lovers for years," she said with a matter-of-fact tone.

Pepsi flew out of Monica's mouth onto the waitress's smock as she approached our table with lobster and steamed broccoli in hand. The waitress almost dropped the huge tray but caught her balance. She was caught off guard. Her eyes stung with relief as she gripped the tray.

"I am so fucking sorry," Monica apologized, clutching her napkin to wipe her mouth as Pepsi still dripped from her chin.

"It's okay." The waitress set each of our meals in front of us. "Can I get you all anything else?" The waitress was still being polite, even though I am sure she wanted to slap Monica in the face.

"No, we are fine," I spoke up. As soon as she exited the table, I looked at Ma, but Monica spoke before me.

"Are you saying Dad was playing you?" Monica was no doubt shocked. She had always looked at my dad as perfect. See, I knew before my dad went to prison that he was in the drug game. Li'l Bo was aware of it as well. But Monica was the baby in the family. Her world was surreal. She had no clue. After Dad was arrested and sent off to jail, kids at her school filled her in with that chapter of our life. And she still didn't come to terms with it until about two years ago. So here was another shocker about our dad landing in her lap. Her mouth was open wide enough to catch flies.

"Yep," Ma answered with a smile. I could tell that she was over it. It was in her past and she had moved on.

"How did you find out?" I asked. To be honest, I was shocked, too. I never knew Dad stepped out on my mom. I guess it is easy to be blind and stupid when you are a kid.

"Well, after he was arrested I found out that her house was raided, too. They found a lot of his guns and drugs in her house. You know the rest, people started talking. I went to the jail livid and he admitted it to me. I was devastated for a while, but I got over it pretty quick. I mean, your dad was a baller. There were millions of bitches that wanted him. But those hoes respected me in the streets, and I never knew. He had them in check. I never had any drama when it came to other females. Your dad treated me like a queen and he put his family first, but he like most men: He was a hoe." When she said that, it made me wonder about Hood. He was a baller with plenty of cash. I'm sure the hoes were after him, too, but he just better not let me find out, because I would cut a bitch quick about my man.

"So what did Suzie have to say? No, forget that, I know you beat her down." I had to know. Hairstylist or not, she should have got it.

"Hell no, I didn't beat her down." She looked at me like I was crazy. "Shit, I never said anything to her about it. I know you think I'm stupid. But I was so caught up with your dad going to prison, I just kinda washed my hands of it. My main concern became how was I gonna take care of my kids. I'm sure your father told her that I knew."

"So you just let her walk away like that? Forgive the slut that sleeps with your man while doing your hair?" I was tripping off that 'cause I would have beat that hoe down.

"Now I did not say I forgave her. Don't get it twisted. But I don't hate her, either. That shit was too long ago. Hell, it ain't like she was the only one. What was I gone do, fight off all the groupies in Detroit?" She hunched her shoulders. I guess she had a point. "But when I thought about going to her to get my hair done, my feelings started rushing back and I said to myself, 'Fuck that bitch. She ain't gettin' in my head.'"

Monica and I busted out laughing. "I know, right." Monica held up her hand and slapped five with Ma.

"Speaking of your dad, on my last visit to see him he told me that his lawyer had filed an appeal on his behalf trying to get his sentence reduced."

"Wow, really?" I was too excited. Since he had been locked up, I had no thoughts of him being released because his convictions left no room for that. I wondered how possible it could be. "How long before he knows?"

"Well, they told him it could take up to a year before he can find out anything. The attorney said the process is long."

I looked over at Monica. She had tears welling up in her eyes. She was sensitive when it came to discussing him being locked away. Visits with him down at the prison were so emotionally hard for her. She struggled daily with his incarceration.

"What's wrong, Monica?" I fought not to soften. I wanted to stay strong and hopeful.

"Nothing," she sniffled. "I just never thought it would be any chance Daddy would ever be released." She picked up another clean napkin and wiped at her tears. "This just gives me hope. When Li'l Bo died, I thought we had lost the last man of our family." I wrestled back the tears.

"I know what you mean. I have been thinking a lot about Li'l Bo," Ma confessed, out of the blue. Her face suddenly flooded with tears. Her pain made my heart drop and my throat tighten. I took a swig from my drink. Both of their open emotions were wearing on me. This was supposed to be a happy lunch. It was quickly turning into a lunch of tears.

"Ma, are you okay? Why haven't you said anything? You know

you can always talk to Monica or me about anything. Especially this. We are your open ears."

"I know. I just didn't want to worry you two with this. But my heart has been so heavy." All of a sudden she let out a gut-wrenching cry that she quickly tried to control. Monica and I looked at each other, our faces wet with tears. We had no idea our mother was in pain. How had we missed her signs? The answer was clear: We both were wrapped up in our own shit when she needed us. I wrapped my arm around her shoulders and pulled her close. Monica reached across the table to hold both of Ma's hands in hers.

"I'm so sorry that I have not been there for you, Ma," Monica apologized.

"Me too." I followed suit with an apology, feeling like shit. "Together we will be there. You can always call me no matter what time it is. Our family comes first. You know that," I reconfirmed. I never wanted that to be misunderstood.

"Look, I know you two love me, but I have to be strong for myself. Any stress can cause me to relapse. But don't worry, I just got back into my therapy sessions. And yes, I'm still clean, if you are wondering. I plan to remain that way. This is why I stressed this lunch today. I wanted to let you both know how I was feeling and what my plan of action was." She looked at us both and smiled. We had her back. "What I need from you is your love and support. That will give me the strength I need to get through this. It means the world to me having you two there."

My heart was beating so fast. The thought of her relapsing was more than I could bear. But the fact that she had admitted it and was seeking help showed me that she was a past addict who was not trying to hide or deceive. There was no question that she really wanted help so we had to be there for her. Monica looked as though the wind had been knocked from her. I would have to be strong for her. She took it the hardest when Ma had been addicted. She was what you call a "Mommy's baby." But something told me that we would get through this.

"If you need anything else, just holla at me. I know you started your therapy sessions again, but I also want to get you a personal counselor. I have the perfect person in mind. Would you be willing to see an additional person?" Normally, convincing her to do something could prove difficult.

Smiling, she answered, "Of course I will do whatever it takes to keep that monkey off my back. I love my new life." I knew she meant every word. Sincerity was all over her face.

"Another thing. We all need a vacation, the whole family. So in the next couple of months, as soon as things slow down, we going somewhere to relax in the sun. Any suggestions?" I looked at them both.

"Hawaii, baby," Ma suggested. "I can't wait to learn to hula." She moved her hips a little from side to side.

"Heck yeah, me too." Monica had perked back up and was grinning. All she ever talked about was vacation.

"Hawaii it is, then. I'll call my travel agent and book it."

As we finished our food, we talked about how we missed Li'l Bo. All the fun memories of him made us laugh. He was loved and we would miss him always, but we had to learn how to keep on living. Li'l Bo would not want his death to destroy us, especially since we were finally getting our family back on a positive track. I knew he was in heaven smiling every time he looked down and saw Ma clean from the drugs and in good health. We would keep our family together in honor of him. And I personally would not fail anyone else in our family.

Chapter 20

After having lunch with Ma and Monica, I stopped by the salon and helped Rochelle count the inventory. Every month we did an inventory check to be sure all products were adding up the way they should. Not that we had ever experienced a problem or did not trust anyone in the salon. It's just that I personally found it easier than waiting until the last minute and trying to do everything at one time. Because if the count happened to be out of whack, we would have a harder time figuring out why.

After we finished the inventory, Rochelle convinced me to do her hair so I still ended up staying longer than I planned. But soon as I wrapped up with her, I headed home and boy, was I tired when I got there. When I entered our excessively huge home, I instantly realized that Hood had not arrived. It was around seven so it was still light outside. I was tired as hell, though, so I decided to jump in a hot bubble bath.

Upstairs I grabbed a lighter and strolled over to my Jacuzzi tub. I lit my lemon lavender and harvest scented candles that I had picked up from Yankee Candles. I absolutely loved Yankee Candles. I could easily spend two hundred dollars in there without even blinking an eye. Not only did I supply my house with them, I bought them for Monica and Ma all the time. I had them addicted as well. Within minutes my bathroom and entire bedroom were lit up with the smell of the scents. I poured some vanilla bath beads along with some coconut-scented bubble bath oil before deciding the bath was ready. I climbed into the warm water and got lost in the scent. I closed my eyes and let the warmth of the water cuddle me. I soaked for an hour before realizing I had fallen asleep. I soaped up, dried off, and threw on some Hello Kitty boxers and tank with slippers before going back downstairs.

Opening the fridge, I knew there was no way I was going to cook anything. Ordering pizzas was the only option. I smiled as I reached for the bottle of Merlot I had put in the fridge earlier to catch a chill. With the bottle and a glass in my hand, I went into the den, where I picked up the phone and ordered pizza. The girl on the other end of the phone told me that they were short-staffed and therefore all deliveries were running behind at least two hours. Instead of canceling the order, I said whatever and placed it anyway. That would be about the time Hood would probably arrive anyhow.

After clicking through the channels, I found *Jumping the Broom* on television, and without much thought I decided to watch it. It was not like the television was crawling with good movies. Only forty-five minutes went by before the doorbell rang. I knew it had to be the pizza guy. Rolling my eyes, I sat my flute down on the coffee table and got up. Every time they told me they would be late they showed up early. I was beginning to think they were full of shit. I think they secretly wanted me to cancel my order and that pissed me off. Snatching the door open to say just that, I came face to face with Rico, one of the new guys that was working with Hood. What the fuck was he doing here?

"Aye, what's up? Mya, right?" He looked me straight in the eye and spoke with confidence. I'm sure he saw the question mark on my face.

"Yeah," I slowly answered, still surprised that he was at my door. "Umm, Hood ain't here." I wanted to clear that up so that he could leave.

"Ahh, damn, really." He sort of scratched his head. "Man, I been tryin' to hit that nigga up. He ain't answer a nigga call, though. I really need to speak wit' him ASAP face to face." He looked puzzled. But I could care less about him needing to speak with Hood. I couldn't do shit about that.

"Well, he ain't here," I repeated and started to shut the door. This conversation was over. Hood was not home and he needed to get the fuck off my doorstep. I didn't like or trust any of them niggas anyway.

I had the door almost closed when he asked, "Can I use your bathroom real quick?"

I looked at him like he was crazy. I almost screamed no at him, but I remained calm. "Actually, I'm sort of busy." I continued to close the big-ass door that led into our foyer.

I heard him chuckle a little with a grin. "I know this strange, but it is a long ride back to the hood. And you know these white folks scared of a brotha. If I stop, they might call the cops on a nigga."

He did have a point. I decided this was bougie country where we live. "A'ight, but you need to hurry up. Like I said before, I got shit to do." I used my irritated tone so that he would know I meant business. I stepped aside to let him come inside, then I pointed him in the direction of the bathroom. I headed back to the den to grab my Merlot bottle. I wanted to put it back into the fridge to chill again. It had been sitting out and I didn't want it to get too warm.

As I came out of the den, I almost walked right into Rico. He had used the bathroom quick just as I had told him to. I was glad because I wanted him out. I was starting to feel uncomfortable with his presence.

"Thank you for letting me use your bathroom."

Instead of speaking, I nodded my head and pointed toward the front door, which for some reason seemed so far away. Rico turned toward the door but stopped. Suddenly my heart started to race for some reason. Why had I let this nigga in my house? Was I that stupid?

"Can I have a drink?" I could not believe his nerve. He had to be kidding! How many times did I have to tell him to leave?

Now I was nervous as hell, but I tried not to show it. "Look, Rico, you need to leave. You being here is not a good idea. Hood would not approve of this." I thought the mention of Hood's name would ring a bell for him.

"A'ight, ma. I'm out." He turned to walk away. I could not believe he had the gall to call me ma like I was some trick out on the street and not Hood's wife. Without warning, Rico turned around and wrapped me tightly in his arms. Dumbfounded, I pushed him off me.

"What the fuck is your problem? Don't you ever touch me!"

Rico pushed me hard into the wall. The look on his face was of evil and lust at the same damn time. I knew what was coming next so I sprang into action. I would not let him touch me. My Merlot bottle went to his face. Blood immediately poured from where I'd cut him.

He screamed out from the pain. "Bitch!" His hands went to his face and touched the blood. I stood in my spot as my chest heaved up and down. I started to rush him again because I knew I had to fight. His fist met my face with a punch that dazed me. I still had a piece of the bottle in my hand so I went at him with it. He was much stronger than me so he wrestled me to the ground. He snatched at my tank and I heard it rip. I screamed out Hood's name. In that moment I felt so bad for the way I had treated him. I needed him here to protect me. Where was he?

When I felt Rico rip my bra off, I sprang back into defense mode. I took my bloody hands and stuck my fingers into Rico's eye sockets. He yelped out in pain with profanities. I felt the finality when he wrapped his strong hands around my throat. I could not move, and memories of Phil choking me quickly clouded my mind. This time I knew I would die. I had nothing to fight back with. There was no gun hidden in my ankle area and I could not break his grasp. Tears ran down my face as I lay still. I could feel death slowly taking me. Rico's face was starting to black out.

But all of a sudden I felt air coming back into my lungs. I was coughing and trying hard to pull in more of that air when I realized Rico was no longer on top of me.

I pulled myself up and saw Hood on top of Rico beating him in the face with his beloved nine-millimeter. Hood continued to beat him until he was unconscious. Turning around, Hood crawled over to me asking me if I was okay. I was shaking with fear as Hood wrapped his arms around me. I cried, feeling safe in my husband's arms.

"Hood," I screamed out as I watched Rico rise up and go for the gun on his hip.

Hood immediately turned around and pumped two shots into Rico's skull. Rico dropped back to the floor with a thud.

"It's okay, baby. That nigga fo sho dead now. Ain't no comin' back for him." He kissed me on the forehead. I stared at Rico's lifeless body that lay on my hall floor and silently thanked God that Hood had come to my rescue.

Chapter 21

It had been weeks since the incident with Rico. To clean up the mess Hood had wrapped the body in plastic and taken it to an undisclosed place where he chopped the body up and fed the parts through a weed eater. After that, we moved on like nothing ever happened. However, I expressed to Hood that I no longer felt comfortable in our home so we decided to put our house on the market at the end of the year. Word on the street was that Rico was missing. Dontae and Silk had been looking high and low trying to locate their partner. Their biggest problem was that they were not from Detroit so the streets were on shutdown when they asked for answers. Hood of course joined the search when possible, but ultimately focused on his crew.

On my drive to the salon I took in the beautiful day. The sun was shining, people were out and about. I felt good. I almost hated to turn off the ignition when I pulled up to the salon bumping David Ruffin's "Missing You Part 1." Inside the salon I spoke to Pam, who was on the phone scheduling appointments. She covered the receiver of the phone and greeted me.

"What's up, Mya."

"Nothing ready to get it in." I beamed. She grinned and nodded her head and then went back to her call. Instead of going to my station, I headed straight toward Rochelle's. To my surprise

Dontae was in there. They were giggling and talking like two love-birds. But I could feel both their eyes on me as I made my entrance.

"Oh hey, girl." Rochelle spoke, blowing gum bubbles as if she had no cares in the world.

"Aye, Mya." Dontae spoke. How dare his punk ass speak to me that way? I knew he could do better than "aye." Niggas these days, I swear, no respect. Just plain assholes.

"Hey" was all I managed with an obvious attitude. "Holla at me later when you have time, Rochelle." I turned and walked away. I had no conversation for Dontae; his whole crew was foul to me.

Not even ten minutes after I left Rochelle's station, she walked into mine.

"Girl, why you run outa there like that."

"I ain't run," I lied.

"Shit, girl, you was outa there when you saw Dontae." Rochelle chuckled.

"I just ain't feelin' him. But you already know that," I reminded her.

"Yeah, I know. And I feel you, too. He don't know it yet, but I'm 'bout to chill on that nigga."

"Oh, so you finally see it my way?" I unscrewed the top on a Coke I had pulled out the fridge in our snack area.

"If you say so. That nigga just gettin' on my nerves. I think he tryin' to keep tabs on me. And you know I don't do well with that controlling shit. Hmmph, I will mess around and catch a charge. So to keep from doing that, I came to the conclusion to let him go. Not only that, but sometimes I get this bad vibe when I'm around him. And that is starting to stick out like a sore thumb. I even stopped bringing Tiny around him."

"What he do to make you feel that way?"

"I don't know, Mi. I can't put my finger on it. Just something odd."

"Ummm, cut that nigga off then." I was all for that. Finally she was seeing things my way.

"You know they homeboy Rico still missing? I think Dontae bugging off that shit, too."

"They still don't know where he at?" I played at being clueless. I hated hiding things from Rochelle, but I knew it was for her own good. The less she knew, the better off she would be.

"Nah, nothing." She confirmed what she knew. I was confident that if Dontae suspected anything, he would have let it slip during pillow talk. Dudes had that bad. All of them including Hood.

"Same thing Hood been tellin' me. That's some crazy shit, though. How somebody just gone disappear into thin air? Sound like some bull to me," I commented, knowing he had got exactly what he deserved. Just talking about him caused my insides to cringe but I kept my cool.

"What you bring to eat?" Rochelle looked around like she expected food to be somewhere in sight.

"I ate some waffles at the crib this morning. I ain't had no lunch." I took a swig of my Coke. The coldness caused me to burp. It rolled out of my throat like mild thunder.

"We need to grab some then. It's almost lunchtime." I was just about to agree with her when we heard someone scream, and before we could think, we saw Trina running toward us.

"Teddy is chasing me!" Trina yelped, but her words sounded strangely muffled almost as if she couldn't speak. Getting a good look at her face, I realized why. Her top and bottom lips were swollen. She had a knot on the side of her face that looked like a lemon, she was bleeding from I have no idea where, and both of her eyes were swollen. I was stunned. Rochelle stood up.

Then I heard Teddy talking loud with bass in his voice. He was calling Trina a bitch, ordering her to come to him. My instant reaction was to go for the Ruger that I kept at the shop.

"Help me," Trina screamed as Teddy entered the room, taking huge steps. Rochelle reached out to grab Trina's arm to pull her out of Teddy's reach. But before she could grab her out the way, he reached out and caught Trina by her hair and pulled her to him. He wasted no time yanking Trina to the floor and proceeding to drag her. Rochelle jumped on his back and started punching him and biting him. All the while Trina screamed for help. Rochelle bit into Teddy's shoulder hard and deep. She came up with a piece of his shirt and flesh in her mouth. He screamed out from the pain and threw her to the floor. Rochelle landed at the feet of my styling chair, inches away from hitting her head on the steel part. I ran for my gun.

Within seconds I was back and watched as Trina tried to get up but Teddy kicked her in the side and she screamed out in pain. She rolled over to protect herself while he kicked her again, all while yelling he was going to kill her. By this time my Ruger was locked and loaded. I aimed at my target.

I screamed, "Teddy, get the fuck away from her!"

"Fuck you, bitch," he responded. Looking at him was like watching the Terminator in action. But he should have known better than to call me a bitch. I did not put up with that disrespect. Without further ado, I pulled the trigger and shot him directly in his left butt cheek. Teddy screamed out, jumping up and down like he was dodging firecrackers. Had this been a different situation I would have been cracking up, but right now I was pissed.

"You get the message now, nigga? Now, get the fuck out before the next one hit your punk ass in the head. Don't you never in your fucking life even think about calling me a bitch!" I yelled. From that point on all I seen was the back of Teddy's shirt as he dashed out the salon. Rochelle crawled over to Trina, who had passed out. She screamed for us to dial 911.

While sitting in the waiting area at the hospital to get word from the doctor, Rochelle and I decided that Trina would stay with one of us when she got out of the hospital. More than an hour passed before the doctor came out and told us that Trina was going to be okay but she had a lot of healing to do. She not only had the injuries to her face, but her ribs were bruised. Rochelle and I agreed that this was by far the worst beating that Teddy had administered to Trina. That nigga was Crazy with a capital C. But he would get it together soon enough. I had called Hood and told him everything that had happened. He vowed to handle Teddy for disrespecting me and my business. All I could say was Teddy was gone get a taste of his own medicine but times ten. 'Cause Hood was going to let his ass have it. Served him right. FUCK TEDDY was my final thought on the matter.

Chapter 22

Trina had been out of the hospital for three weeks and she was staying with Rochelle. Rochelle had decided it best she stay with her since she had a flat condo and I had stairs. Because of her badly bruised ribs, Trina couldn't do a lot of climbing. Teddy ended up in ICU after he was severely beaten courtesy of Hood. Last we heard he was still fighting for his life because he had bled internally. This beating had traumatized Trina. She would shake if his name was so much as mentioned in her presence. She had pressed full charges on him with no encouragement from us. According to her, she had had enough and she vowed to get her a gun permit as soon as she was well enough. She said that would gladly bust a cap in him if he came anywhere near her. I seriously doubted he would cross her path after his ICU visit. If he lived.

At the house, Hood was walking around preparing for his deal. It was going down that night. I watched him like a hawk. Instead of eating out, I prepared some fried catfish with coleslaw, hush puppies, and fries. We watched a movie and enjoyed it. Afterwards he started preparing for his mission. Everything had to be intact. I could see the rush on his face. He was ready to get that dough.

"Come here." Hood called me over to him. He had just finished loading his heat. He had two 9mm Glocks and a .35, all three shined like a baby's behind. Watching him suit up with them always turned me on for some reason. My baby was a certified gangster. I walked over to him wondering what was up, because the look on his face was serious. When I was close enough, he reached out and pulled me to him. He looked me in the eyes.

"I know these last couple of months been crazy for us, but I want you to know your words ain't been fallin' on deaf ears. I have been hearing you loud and clear. After tonight I'm really gonna walk away from the game." I didn't know whether to smile or not. Was he serious? Would he really give it up just like that?

"Just like that. You gone walk away?" I searched his eyes. I wanted truth.

"Yeah, I mean I got to tie up some loose ends. Make sure everything straight 'cause if it ain't right, it could start a war on the street. But I kinda already started that a couple of weeks ago, small stuff. My plan is to pass the rock to Pablo. Li'l nigga been working hard for a long time alongside me and Pig. He put in mad work. He earned it. I just gotta clear him for all the contacts and a few other things. But that's it for me. I'ma settle down and be here for you. Just like you been askin'. Maybe we can travel the world or some before we start our family." He grinned.

"Oh, Hood." I jumped in his arms and wrapped my legs around his waist with so much force he stumbled back. "I love you, babe," I whispered in his ear, then gently bit the tip of his earlobe.

"I love you, too," he cried out in pure ecstasy.

At that moment he couldn't have been sexier to me. Hood gripped my ass so tight I felt myself burning with desire. I threw my tongue down his throat. His mouth was so warm I moaned with each stroke. Unable to control himself any longer, Hood walked me over to the kitchen counter and sat me down. He ripped my shirt off and exposed my ample breasts and feasted for dear life. I needed him right then, so I forcefully undid his belt buckle and pushed his pants down. I arched my back and he entered his safe place and burst into flames within minutes. Damn, we were made for each other. For the next two hours we went round for round until sleep claimed us.

I woke up to the ringtone that belonged to Rochelle and an empty spot in the bed that belonged to Hood. He had left for his deal and instead of waking me up, he let me sleep. I thanked him for that because I was still exhausted.

"Hello," I breathed into the phone.

"Dang, chick, what took you so long to answer? I done called you twice."

I pushed myself up in the bed. "I musta been out like a light then. I was asleep. What's up, though? You done woke me up now."

"Girl, this nigga Dontae's ass is crazy. I done popped off on his ass up in here."

"Oh, snap, what he do?" I knew this was going to be good. Rochelle was a firecracker: It didn't take much to piss her off. Sometimes she tries to hold her tongue when it comes to her man, but that ain't easy for her, either.

"This dude got the fucking nerve to tell me to put Trina out. Now, Mya, who this nigga think he talkin' to? I went ham up in here."

"You mean he just walked up to you and said put her out."

"Hell, yeah, like he runnin' shit up in my crib. I ask that nigga did he pay any bills up in this motherfucker? And I made it clear that this my house and Trina will stay until I say go. Then I got his shit that he been storing at my crib and told that nigga to hit the bricks. That's it. It's over, not that we had nothing that real." Rochelle could be cold like that sometimes. She did not play.

"What he say? He didn't act up, did he?" I was laughing on my end. I knew that sometimes dudes got crazy when you dissed them and threw them out.

"At first he was tryna say he was sorry but I didn't wanna hear it. I told you I was gettin' tired and suspicious of his ass anyway. Some 'bout him ain't right. He be making sneaky-ass moves and shit. That nigga Silk ain't right neither. He be callin' Dontae at strange times havin' him make moves. I don't know. I just get bad vibes. For instance, this morning he was in the bathroom on the phone with somebody. He was whispering, but I know I heard him say Hood's name at least twice." Rochelle was popping her mouth and talking a mile a minute.

"Hood?" After I heard his name, she had my undivided attention. I was all ears.

"Mya, I'm sure that is what I heard him say. I just couldn't make out anything else he was saying. Like I said that nigga be makin' them sneaky-ass moves. How well does Hood know them niggas anyway? You know they just popped up in Detroit out the clear blue? They asses ain't from here." My mind was going wild. I didn't trust them, either. And who would Dontae be on the phone talking with that he had to whisper Hood's name? Hood was with them right now. I wondered if I should worry.

"He met them through Rob and some other connections. That is all I know. But you know Hood screen niggas off top. You know how he can be when it comes to trust. Besides, he is meeting with them niggas right now. They got a big deal going down tonight." I was a little nervous but Hood could take care of himself; that I was sure of. If them niggas were rotten, they would deal with me.

"I know 'cause Dontae was talkin' about finishing up then coming back to work things out with me. After I done called him every motherfucker and son of a bitch in the book. Ain't that crazy? But I told that nigga he better not bring his butt back over here. I got my pistol waiting for his psycho ass if he do," Rochelle mouthed.

"They ass betta be legit anyway. I'ma talk with Hood tonight when he come home. What are you and Trina doing?"

"Nothin'. Trina just hooked us up some stir-fry and butter rolls. Mya, it's off the hook! I'm about to go in. Why don't you come over? We got plenty. I just gave Tiny her bath and put her down for the night."

"Nah I'ma chill. I ain't hungry anyway. I fried some fish earlier. I'ma take me a shower and turn in early."

"A'ight then, I'll see you in the morning at the salon."

"No doubt." I hung up and threw the covers off me. Rochelle

had really got me to wondering about Dontae and Silk. I already knew they were not to be trusted. Rico had proved that to me. But he had paid dearly for it with his life. Hood had been planning this deal for months, though. Other than Rico's sudden betrayal, I'm sure he had no reason to doubt them. Besides, they had already had several successful deals since connecting. Maybe I was being paranoid. A shower and a shot of Hennessey would ease my mind. This damn drug life. Stressful.

Chapter 23

My sleep had been miserable because I tossed and turned most of the night. I couldn't remember dreaming, but I was definitely asleep. When I finally opened my eyes in the morning, I was exhausted from fighting for comfort during my restless night. As soon as my eyelids opened, I realized I was turned facing Hood's side of the bed. His spot was as empty as it had been before I dozed off the night before. I knew immediately that he had not been home because his pillows were still intact. Something was odd. Turning over on my right side, I reached out and grabbed my cell off the nightstand. The screen showed ten a.m. and I had no missed calls.

Either something was wrong or Hood had lost his damn mind. He knew he had better call me. Especially with it being another day. Unlocking my phone, I pressed Hood's name on the screen. It didn't ring once; his phone went straight to voice mail. My mind told me to remain calm, but my heart skipped at least one beat. The conversation that I had with Rochelle the night before quickly replayed in my mind. Then my house phone rang and that brought me back to reality. No one ever called me on that damn thing. I had already decided not to answer. But what if it was Hood? I mean, he never called that phone, but I was not taking any chances. I yanked the covers back and sprinted to the cordless phone that was only there for show.

"Hello." I was out of breath from my sudden fast-paced movement. To my dismay it was a telemarketer. I must have called that lady a thousand bitches before ending the call and throwing the phone to the floor. Out of all the days they could call this house, they picked this one. My nerves were getting the best of me.

Then it hit me to call Rochelle to see if Dontae had made good on his promise to come back and fix their relationship. Rochelle's cell rang at least eight times before she finally picked up.

"Dang, Ro, what took you so long." I was agitated.

"Oh, I was just in the back getting some shampoo. What's up?" she asked, sounding like she didn't have a care in the world.

"Ummm, did Dontae come back through last?"

"Hell, naw. He ain't stupid. Why? What's wrong? You sound stressed."

Hearing that Dontae had not showed back up did little to ease my mind. I needed her to find out where he was. "Look, I need you to call him and see if he will tell you where they at."

"Mya, now you know I ain't tryin' do all that. You know the situation. Did you hear anything I said last night? I am through with his ass."

"Rochelle, do this for me, a'ight. Hood didn't come home last night. So just do it!" I sort of yelled. I did not mean to get upset at her.

"Oh snap, why you ain't tell me?" Rochelle sounded apologetic. "A'ight, look, I'ma call Dontae and hit you right back." She hung up. I felt bad for yelling at her. I should have told her from the start.

In literally less than a minute my phone was ringing back. That's when I knew something was wrong. If she had gotten Dontae on the phone, it would take longer for her to get back to me.

"Hello," I answered the phone.

"He didn't answer," she replied in a soft tone. She knew that was not the answer I was waiting for.

"Damn!" I screamed. "Something ain't right, Rochelle." My

voice turned shaky and tears slid down each side of my cheeks. Chills were shooting up and down my spine.

"Well, we gone find out. I'm 'bout to have Pam cancel all my appointments and leave her in charge. I'm on my way." Before I could protest, she had hung up. Not knowing what else to do, I forced my weak legs to take me back to my bed, where I stayed in silence until Rochelle arrived.

———◦◉◦———

Three days had gone by and I had not heard one word from Hood. I was completely sick with grief. I was not eating and had lost like five pounds. The first two days Rochelle and I went hard on the streets trying to find out something. I visited all of his trap houses and spoke with his workers one by one. All of them claimed to know nothing or had heard nothing from Hood or Pablo. According to them they were still waiting on orders of what to do about reup. I almost told them to shut down. But realistically, I knew that would not be a good idea because the streets would just get crazier. And I knew that Hood would not want me to do that, so I stepped up. Hood never really shared his business with me when it came to trapping. Luckily for him, some things I knew from just watching. Fortunately, knowing how to reup was one of them, so I did it.

I also made it clear that even though Hood was not back yet, shit needed to stay tight. I spread the word to them that Hood had a lookout guy that would murk they asses on sight if there was any problems, especially shortages. That lookout guy was me. And rest assured, with my man missing I was on edge, so it wouldn't take much for me to bust the nine-millimeter.

Handling that situation had drained me. I was depressed. Mom, Monica, and Imani came out to the house and stayed a couple of days. They tried to get me to eat, but I just couldn't. The knot in my throat would not allow food to go down. But I was drinking fluids so that was keeping me alive. I was at a loss for words. I needed a plan and I didn't know where to start. Hood had kept me in the dark about this huge deal. Not that I blamed him. I had been on his back so much about getting out of the game. There was no way he could have discussed it with me even if he wanted to. The only thing I was interested in hearing was that he was done with that life. I did not regret encouraging him to walk away. Now I wished more than ever that he had listened to me. I wondered what had gone wrong and why he had not come back. We learned he was not the only one missing. No one had heard from Dontae, Pablo, or Silk. The three of them had all but vanished from the city of Detroit. But I knew somebody knew something. In the hood no one ever just disappears. That was considered impossible.

Mom and Monica were preparing to go home since Rochelle had come by and would be staying with me for a while. I had tried to get all of them to go home because I wanted my space. Not giving me a choice, they vowed someone would have to stay with me until I started eating again. So I had made up my mind to eat something just to get Rochelle out, too. She was in the kitchen whipping up some chicken noodle soup. She figured I could at least get that down since I complained of this huge knot I had in my throat, even though I was aware it was only stress.

I headed to the den to lie down on the sofa. It was six o'clock so I decided to watch the news. I hardly ever got a chance to watch the news because normally I was still at the salon. But occasionally when I made it home in time I would watch. Plopping my weak, foodless body down on the sofa facing the flat screen on the wall, I grabbed the remote and scanned through the channels until I found it. Maybe this could take my mind off Hood for at least a few minutes, but I doubted it. As soon as I stopped on the station, "Breaking News" flashed across the screen.

Two dead bodies had been found shot up behind an abandoned building. Apparently the bodies had been there for at least three days. The owner of the building had showed up to check for squatters. She had been having trouble with them trespassing in her building. When she opened the door, she got sick from the stench escaping the building. She followed the smell and found the bodies. The news said that it looked to be a drug-related issue that went bad. I screamed out. I didn't even hear the sound as it left my mouth. I tried to get up to find Rochelle. I felt off balance and started to sway. Rochelle almost bumped into me as she entered the den.

"What is wrong, Mya? What happened?" Her eyes searched mine for answers.

For a couple of seconds I could not speak. I pointed at the television. "They found them. Look. He is dead." As I said those unthinkable words, I collapsed into Rochelle's arms. I could not believe this was happening again. Li'l Bo murdered and now Hood, my own husband.

Rochelle fixed her gaze on the television while trying to hold me up. "No, Mya, it ain't him." I heard her words, but they did not register with me. I was too devastated. Rochelle tried to lift me up on my feet. "It ain't him," she repeated again. This time I heard her.

"Rochelle, they just announced it. I heard them say it," I managed through my clouded vision of tears.

"No, it's Dontae and Pablo, they just said their names." I slowly turned back toward the television, but I was having a hard time seeing the screen. Somehow I took one of my hands and wiped my tears away as best I could. My vision was still a bit blurry but I was able to see Dontae and Pablo's pictures as they flashed across the screen.

I sucked in a sigh of relief. She was right, it was not Hood, but that still did not change the fact that he was missing. Where in the hell was he? I wanted to know. And then a light came on. Where was Silk at? He was a major part of the deal. If there was no Hood or Silk, had they both been kidnapped or something?

Rochelle got me settled back on the couch and eventually I ate some of her homemade chicken noodle soup. To my surprise I ate the whole bowl and it was so good, I even asked for seconds. I did not realize how hungry I was until I started eating. The food also gave me back my thought process. For the first time since

Hood had disappeared I could see things for what they were. The fact of the matter was I was all Hood had and I needed to be strong for him, which meant I had to be in good health in order to help him. Starving myself and crying all day was not the way to handle this type of situation. I understood that better than most. I had conquered the trenches before. I had to be a solider, be the bad bitch that I was capable of being. I had to put a plan into action to find my man. And I knew just who I needed to speak with to help me with a major question. It was Lester, my dad. He may have been behind bars, but he knew everything about the streets. I needed to know what could cause a dealer as major as Hood was in Detroit to just turn up missing.

I mean I was not stupid. I knew that Hood was not King Kong, but he was heavy in the streets. There were only two major suppliers in the Detroit area: Hood and this other dealer who went by Tonic. Tonic and Hood had no beef. They kept the streets peaceful because the last time things got out of hand, the city was almost shut down. So Hood kept his side supplied and Tonic did the same. Together they kept the streets jumping. I had personally contacted Tonic the first day and he assured me that he had nothing to do with this. The streets seemed to have the same question I had. Where was Hood? It was time I got some answers.

Chapter 24

I was up first thing the next morning. It was Saturday and I could make that trip down to see my dad. My timing for figuring out what I had to do could not have been more perfect, since it was visiting day. I got up, jumped in the shower, then threw on a pair of khaki Polo shorts, a pink-and-white-striped Tommy Hilfiger V-neck tee, and a pair of all-white Polo shoes. After throwing my hair in a soft ponytail, I headed downstairs.

I knew Rochelle was up because I could smell the bacon all the way up the stairs. It was her mission to keep some food in me. "Good morning," I said.

She had her head in the fridge digging out the orange juice. When she turned around, she looked shocked when she saw me fully dressed. Not that I was surprised; I mean, just the day before I looked like hell. My hair had been flying everywhere and I had one sock on, the other off. I was a mess. "So you up early and dressed today?" She smiled.

"Yep, I am on a mission." I reached for a cup from the cabinet. That orange juice in her hand looked cold and good. My throat begged for a swallow.

"Where are you going? The look on your face says mission." She set the Tropicana down on the counter then headed toward the skillet that she was using to fry the bacon.

"Well, I need to make this four-hour trip down to the prison to see my dad." I poured the orange juice in my glass.

"Dang, Mya, you sure you up for that drive?" She sounded concerned.

"Yeah, I'm good. Besides, I need to do this."

"A'ight, I'ma roll with you. Matter fact I'll drive."

"Naw, I'm good. Why don't you just go into the salon today and make sure everything is okay. I'll be back tonight."

"You sure, Mya?" She watched me as she removed the bacon from the skillet.

"I'm telling you I got this. I done made this trip millions of times." I took a huge swallow of juice. It felt free sliding down my throat. I was thirsty as hell.

"Okay, but I want you to eat first. I don't need Ms. Marisa cursing me out 'cause your grown ass ain't ate nothin'."

"I know, right." We both laughed, then I polished off the rest of my juice.

After gassing up my silver Mercedes, I hit the highway. I fought back the tears and thought about Hood the entire way. When I arrived, I could see that everybody's family had decided to show up today. The waiting area was packed. It had been about a minute since I had been down to see Dad. I had been so busy I just could not pull myself away, but we talked on the phone whenever he called. He spent most of his time calling Ma. They had gotten really close since she had been clean. It was just like they had been before he got locked up. They were always laughing and joking. In love is what they were. Through it all, that had not changed.

For a minute I started to get scared. I thought I would not be able to see him. My gut feared something was wrong because after I signed in, it took them a while to take me back. Even after they had taken back the other family members, I was left in the waiting area. I thought that maybe he was on lockdown again. But finally a tall, dark, bald-headed guard with a mouth full of gold came out to get me. Relief washed over me as he escorted me back.

To my surprise Lester was already sitting behind the glass

when I got back there. He already had the phone in his hand and a smile spread across his face. I didn't hesitate to pick my phone up before sitting all the way down.

"Hey, Dad." I sounded just like a little girl whenever I talked to him. Even though he was behind a glass, seeing him always made my load seem lighter.

"Look at my princess. You look more like your mother every day. How you doing, baby girl?"

Tears instantly started to roll down my cheeks. I always went there with the intent to stay strong and not cry. But I hated seeing him caged like some fucking animal. Talking to him from behind a glass. I mean, who ever thought that shit up? He was no monster, just my dad, and I wanted to feel his embrace. I swear it tore at my soul.

"Come on, baby girl, not the crocodile?" He made jokes about my tears. I chuckled as I wiped them away.

"I'm sorry, Daddy. You know how I get."

He nodded with a grin, letting me know that he understood.

"I almost thought they were not going to let me see you. What took you so long to come out?"

"Oh, it was nothing. My lawyer had showed up. He needed me to sign some papers for this appeal thing. They were taking me back to my cell when they got the call that I had a visitor, so they had to prepare me for the visit. Sorry. I did not mean to worry you."

"It's cool. How is the appeal going? What does the lawyer say? Are things lookin' good?" I fired questions at him.

"Well, we're hoping. At this point that is all we can do. But I stay positive. 'Cause hope is the only thing you got in this shithole." He looked around as if to confirm his statement. "Anyway, I'm glad you came down today. I swear you can read my mind or something. Every time I need you to come, you just pop up. I was going to call you last night to see if I could get you out here ASAP. But these niggas got us locked down early with no phone time." He looked annoyed.

Him saying ASAP had gotten my attention. Red flags went up. "What's wrong, Dad?"

He looked over his shoulder as he watched the guard who had just walked behind him. But the guard moved on. He put his lips closer to the phone to muffle his sounds. This way he would not be loud enough to be heard by anyone on his side of the window. "I know all about Hood missing."

My heart instantly started racing. "You do? How did you find out?" Again tears took over my face. I just could not control them so I decided, fuck it. "Daddy, I don't know where he is or what happened but it's been three days." I continued to cry.

I could see that he was hurting watching me cry. He again turned around and watched the guard's movement. When he saw that he was out of hearing range, he gave me his attention. Again he put his mouth close to the phone. "Mya, listen to me, the streets are talkin' to us up in here. You know we get the information that y'all can't get on the streets. Listen to me carefully, Hood is hooked up with these guys named Dontae, Rico, and Silk, right?" I was dumbfounded he actually knew their names. This was going to be bad. I just nodded.

"I don't know what happened to Hood, but these dudes are involved. They work for this guy named Monty. Why they set this up I don't know, but that deal was never gone happen and this guy Monty is behind it all."

I was confused. Who was this Monty character? "Are you saying Hood was set up?" I had to be clear.

"Yeah. But I don't know why. These dudes are all from New York. Now it could be because Hood is major in this area. Sometimes out-of-towners come into a city just to make a major score. I don't know. But this Monty has all the answers you need and he is in town. He has been here for three days—tomorrow night he leaves and will probably never return. Once he is off this turf, you may never hear from him again."

Dad was right: Whoever this Monty was, I had to find him. "I gotta go, Dad," I said into the receiver. There was no time to waste.

"Wait, Mya, you be careful. These types of niggas are grimy and heartless. Killing to get what they want is their primary game. So expect nothing but be ready for anything. 'Cause if anything happens to you, I will have dead bodies on the streets of Detroit all the way up to New York. And I won't stop until I feel satisfied." I looked him in the eyes and I knew he meant it. I assured him I would be careful and I was out. Time was an imperative and preserving life was key.

The drive back was long but it gave me time to think and now some things were adding up. The fact that I never trusted any of those guys—Dontae, Rico, or Silk—was confirmed. I could never put my finger on it, but I got bad vibes from them from the very first moment Hood introduced us. Even Rochelle had begun to have some suspicions about them. Hood should have cut them all off after he had killed Rico for trying to rape me. But I guess he figured he had taken care of the problem. Clearly he had been wrong. Those bastards had set him up from jump. But why?

Poor Rob. I wondered if he and Hood were both supposed to die on that trip. Dad said that all those guys were from New York and that is where Rob had been killed. Hood had not been able to finish up that deal because it went wrong. I hated to even think it, but I had warned him about them. That didn't matter now, though. I had to deal with the situation at hand. Where was Monty? I needed to find him so that he could personally tell me what happened to Hood.

Chapter 25

Finally I had touched back down in Detroit. It had just gotten dark outside. I had no time to ponder over any one thing, so it was important that I make haste with the time I did have. The first thing I decided to do was run by to check on Monica and Ma. I had not seen them since they had left my house the day before. They had called Rochelle first thing this morning to check on me, so I just wanted to show them my face just to assure them that I was doing all right. I also wanted to see them before shit got real hectic in my life. I was about to hit the streets looking for answers. During the drive back I had made the decision not to share the information with them about that Monty guy. It would have only increased their worry for me.

I turned on the block where Ma and Monica still lived at River Place Luxury Condos and saw five squad cars parked outside. That was unusual to me. I had never even seen a cop in the building before. River Place was like one of the safest complexes downtown. Something had to be wrong. I wondered what was going on. Parking my Mercedes next to Monica's Dodge Charger, I got out and hit my locks as I made my way inside the building. There were a few people standing around in a small huddle in the lobby area, which also was unusual. Instead of stopping to question what was going on in the building I walked over and pushed the elevator button, climbed inside, and selected the necessary button to take me up.

The elevator stopped and I attempted to step out into the hallway. I immediately heard Monica screaming at the top of her lungs. I turned toward their condo to see them standing inside the doorway; the door was wide open. There were like three detectives struggling to help my ma hold Monica up. But she continued to scream as well as pull away from them. I ran into the crowd. I wanted to see my sister and find out what had her distraught.

This short, dark-skinned detective grabbed me by my waist and picked me up, placing me back out into the hallway.

"Put me down, dumbass!" I yelled. I almost slapped him but somehow I contained myself.

"Ma'am, this is a crime scene, you cannot just go in there." I could smell the two-hour-old coffee coming off his sour tongue. I rolled my eyes at him out of pure disgust.

"What do you mean?" My eyes roamed him from head to toe with much attitude. "What fucking crime? That is my sister!" I pointed in Monica's direction. The word *crime* sent my heart racing; the only thing that kept my sanity was that I saw Ma and Monica standing before me. Finally Ma broke away and came into the hallway.

"Please let her come in. She is my daughter." She briefly touched my shoulder. But she was shaking like a leaf. And I could easily tell her eyes were swollen from crying. She looked sick.

"Tell me what is going on, Ma?" I threw my hands up in utter frustration. Nobody had once tried to tell me that. But Monica's next scream completely filled me in.

"Get me my baby back. Please!"

I looked from the officer, then at Mom, and right away my eyes swelled with tears. "Where is Imani?" I asked. I could barely ask the question. My breathing became shallow.

"She's been kidnapped, Mya," Ma answered, followed by crying.

I almost fainted. I stumbled back, but the little stank-breath detective and another white detective caught me before I fell. I had to digest what she had just said. There is no way someone had taken my niece. Who? Why? These were the questions burning at my soul.

I ran back into the apartment straight into Monica's arms. We hugged each other and cried. I was sick with grief, but I snapped out of it. I dried my tears because I had to be strong for Monica. "Don't worry. I will find her for you, Monica." I looked her in her eyes and she was not okay. She just cried more.

"She took her, Mya. Please go get Imani back," she pleaded with me. My heart ached for her.

"She. Who is she?" I asked, looking from Monica to the detectives.

Then Ma came up behind. "I am so sorry, Mya. I didn't know she would do that. I thought she just come by to see us and she—" I cut her off.

Shaking my head from left to right and rubbing my temples I tried to think clear but confusion was clouding me in more ways than one. And frustration was the enemy. "Who the fuck is SHE!" I yelled at Mom.

"Felicia. Charlene's old friend," Ma finally said.

The sound of Felicia's name caused the room to spin. Why in the world Felicia would kidnap Imani? Revenge was the only answer I could come up with. She was mad about me beating her up. She had said it was not over. A statement I quickly brushed off because I would have never guessed that she would do something like this.

I needed to know what happened. I pulled Ma to the living room, away from the detectives.

"Ma, I need you to tell me. Are you sure it was Felicia?" I needed to be sure. I knew she was familiar with Felicia. Back in the day, Charlene would bring her over from time to time when I would do her hair. Plus we all went to school together and Felicia also grew up in the Brewster.

"Yeah, it was her. I remembered her and she knew I did. She came by saying she was supposed to be meeting up with Monica."

Now that was a surprise to me. I never knew anything about Monica and Felicia being friends. So this was new information to me.

I turned to Monica. "Monica, did you know she was coming by?" She shook her head no. I turned my attention back to Ma. "Did she say what about?"

"No, she never said. Monica was not here, she had that meeting today for her SATs. So I told her I would let Monica know she came by but she asked me could she wait for her. She showed me this bottle of Moët that they were supposed to sip on. I told her that Monica was not allowed to drink. She laughed and said it was really for herself. So I let her in. She offered me some of the Moët while we waited on Monica. I grabbed some glasses, she poured us a drink. Right away she asked me how Imani was doing. I told her fine and that she was taking a nap. Before long we were drinking the Moët and I started to feel a little sleepy. I did not think anything was strange since I had been up since this morning. I thought maybe I was still sleepy. The next thing I know, I was waking up and Monica was here asking me where was Imani. I told her she was taking a nap. Monica said she had already been in the back. Puzzled, I sat up and that is when I remembered I had been drinking with Felicia and I could not remember her leaving. I looked on the table and the Moët bottle we were drinking out of was gone and so was Felicia's glass. That's when I knew."

I was dumbfounded that this bitch had deliberately come over here and taken my niece. She had planned it and everything. Not only had she kidnapped my niece, she drugged my mom.

"Did you tell the cops all this?" I asked. I glanced in the direction of the cops. They were standing around discussing something and writing notes on their little notepads. That was a bunch of bull. I would have Imani back before they could type up their tired report. I slowly rose up off the sofa. I walked over to Monica and hugged her.

I whispered in her ear. "Don't cry, sis. I will get her back, you just hang tight. Trust me." I kissed her on the forehead. Monica looked at me and I knew she believed me.

I told Ma to stay there and take care of Monica and that I would be back.

Back inside my car, I beat my steering wheel. I could not believe the nerve of that bitch. She would curse the day she fucked with me or my family. Now all I had to do was find her, but I had no idea where she was staying. As I laid my head on my steering wheel, my thoughts were flooded with all the past events from the last few days. Shit had gotten really crazy. I thought about everybody in Hood's circle. I saw each of their faces individually. Then it hit me again. Silk was not found with Dontae and Pablo! I needed to find that snake. If I found him, I could find Hood and Felicia. Maybe I would find them together. Silk plotted with Felicia to kidnap Imani and possibly murder Hood? Was there a connection? Either way I needed to find Silk. Felicia was his girl so he knew where to find her.

Silk was also my connection to Monty. Dad said he worked for him. I was going to visit all of them and I was taking hell with me. The one thing I had over Silk was that he was not from Detroit. So I could get the word on where he was hiding out even before I could on Felicia. Niggas had no love for out-of-towners. They would easily give them up if you offered the stacks.

Pulling out my cell phone, I decided to call up one of Li'l Bo's old trap buddies. He could get me any information I wanted from the streets. That is, for the right price, of course, but money was no object. I offered him five racks to get me Silk's location. It took him all of fifteen minutes to call me back with the address where Silk was laying low. My next call was to Big Nick, an old friend of Dad's. Nick could get any piece I needed and it would never be traced. Nick answered on the second ring. It was on.

Arriving at Big Nick's penthouse took me back a couple years to when I had come to visit him to get some guns. I was wowed by the whole scene. It was extravagant in appearance. Italian this and Italian that. His penthouse reminded me of *The Jeffersons* off television. They had a doorman, top-notch security, you name it. The only thing he was missing was the maid. I was impressed, and for me that was hard for anyone to accomplish.

When I arrived at Big Nick's building, he had already notified all necessary building personnel of my arrival. After I checked in at the front desk, a butler took me all the way up to the twelfth floor just as I remembered from the last visit.

Big Nick opened the door up with a glass of Cognac in his hand and I could tell he was already in there, too. I smiled. "I see you gettin' it in."

"Baby girl, you know I gotta stay tipsy. You wanna take a shot," he offered.

"Nah, I'm good. I need to keep my mind clear." All my sorrow rushed to my face. I was fighting to be strong, but the pain was cutting me too deep. I could feel the blood rushing through my veins. My heartbeat was even different, the rhythm was off.

"Hey, hey, what's with da tears." Big Nick sat his glass down and walked over and hugged me. For a moment I lost all my pride. I fell in his arms and cried. His strong embrace made me even more vulnerable with the tears. I felt safe.

"Tell me what happened," he encouraged me.

I straightened up as best I could and tried to fight the tears. "Shit so fucked up right now, Nick."

"Lay it on me." He guided me over to a sofa where I sat down. I needed to sit down; my legs felt like they would give out any minute.

"Well, you know Monica had a baby, Imani . . ." My lips trembled. "Well, she was kidnapped today. Imani was." I wanted to clarify who was missing.

"What the fuck?" Big Nick looked devastated. Rubbing his forehead, he started to pace the room.

"And that is not all." I sniffled. "Hood is missing. I don't know if you have been watching the news? If you heard anything about those dead bodies they found. One of those guys was his homey.

The other, well, I ain't sure what to call him, they were supposed to be doing a deal, though."

Big Nick was still circling the room and rubbing his forehead as if to make some sense out of everything I had laid on him. "Wait now, you say that Imani was kidnapped and Hood went missing while doing a deal?"

"Well, yes. I mean I don't know for sure about Hood but Imani was kidnapped by some bitch who ass I beat a minute back."

"So that was some revenge type shit."

"You can say that."

"Who was these niggas Hood supposed to do the deal with?"

"I don't know much about them besides their names and that they from out of town. I just knew about the deal because I been pressin' Hood about gettin' out the game. Other than that, he don't tell me nothin' about what he do. But I got to find him and Imani before it is too late."

"No doubt. I'ma call up some people and get some leads goin', then we gone hit the street." Big Nick was ready to cause bloodshed on the streets of Detroit. But I wanted to do this alone.

"Look, I appreciate it, but I got to do this alone. I can move better and get into places I need to easier if I'm alone."

"Fuck that." Big Nick looked at me like I was crazy. "I ain't lettin' you go out there alone. These streets are monstrous at the least." He was telling me nothing I did not already know.

And I understood what he was saying, but I had to convince him otherwise. I stood up. "Listen, Nick, I can do this. All I need you to do is supply me with the right heat and I'ma make these niggas feel it." I meant every fucking word. There was about to be hell to pay. "But I tell you what, I will call you if I need your help. Just let me do this by myself."

Big Nick was looking at me like he was not sure if he could trust that I would call him. He knew I was Lester's daughter and that meant I had my own back. "Girl, you just like your daddy," he declared but finally agreed. "Okay, go ahead, but you better hit me if shit get sticky. And I mean that."

"A'ight, I will. I promise." I started searching the room with my eyes. "Now, where is my heat?" We needed to cut the conversation and get down to business. The clock was ticking and my nerves were along with it.

He gave me a killer grin. "I thought you would never ask. Follow me."

I rose up off the sofa and fell into step behind him as we went into the huge room with the pool table. It was the same spot I suited up the last time he hooked me up. Spread out on the pool table before me was some of the heat that I would be using. The table was full of all type of handguns. Big ones. I'm sure he had more orders to fill.

"That is a Smith & Wesson." I picked up the gun. He watched me fake-aim the gun. I wanted to see what my shots would be like. "That weight is just enough so that you can carry it concealed just like you want. Now this here is a Ruger SR45. You gone love this one."

I set the Smith & Wesson down as he passed the Ruger SR45 to me. I already owned a couple of Rugers that Big Nick had supplied me with, but I needed some new heat with new numbers on it. And just like the last time, he came through.

"I think I got just what I need. I'm already strapped wit' a nine," I confirmed.

"Damn, you ain't playin', is you?"

I gave him a look that answered his question, then I suited up. I had to get going. I hugged Big Nick good-bye and promised to call him if I needed him. But truth be told, I had no plans on calling him. I didn't want to involve him in my mess. I would take care of this on my own.

Chapter 26

Before dropping in on Silk, I wanted to change into something more comfortable and darker, which would make me less noticeable. I threw on a pair of black Levi's, a black tee, with some all-black Nike Air Shox. I also decided to change cars. I jumped in Hood's white Bentley Continental; somehow riding in his car made me feel closer to him as I geared up to find out what had happened to him. Jumping inside and firing up the ignition, I almost jumped out of my skin as 2Chainz's "Fuckin' Problems" blasted out of the speakers. I had told him time and time again to turn that shit down when he got out. I guess he never listens. I smiled thinkin' about the way I had just jumped. You would have never thought I was the same chick that had robbed and killed in the past.

When I arrived at the location where Silk was supposed to be staying, I assessed the area then the house once I confirmed the address. The house was a little brick ranch-style flat sitting at the back of a dead-end street. Why would his dumb ass rent a house on a dead-end street? I guess he wanted his enemies to surround him. Stupid. I parked a few houses down on a portion of the street that was dark. Some of the streetlights were out, which worked fine for me; it would be hard to notice much. This area was not the Bentley type: The last thing I needed was for someone to try to steal my only ride or me have to waste a bullet on a fool for trying to carjack me. Either way I had business on this street, so I parked and jumped out.

I made my way around the back in search of the back door. I figured I could ease my way inside without being noticed. Clearly Silk's punk ass was scared of the dark because he had all the lights on in the house. Every room in the house seemed to be lit up. Maybe he had company, but the house was quiet, so he seemed to be alone. Plus the information that I had received said that he would be alone. I was almost to the back door when the ground sucked me in. I had stepped into a big black hole. I almost screamed but I kept my composure and covered my own mouth. I could not believe this cheap-ass dude would not get a hole that deep filled. I could have easily broken my leg, but I caught my balance before putting too much weight on the leg that had been ravaged by the hole. After dusting myself off, I made my way to the back door.

I reached to my waist and pulled out the Ruger for protection. Niggas be thinking they tough so the heat was reassurance to get some to act right.

I had a key in my back pocket that opened most door locks, but before reaching for it, instinct told me to try the doorknob. I reached out and touched it, then slowly and very lightly turned it. The knob twisted all the way. The door was unlocked! I could not believe my luck. Did he think he was in a gated community? Being this stupid, he deserved what he got.

Stepping inside the back door put me directly into the kitchen. Talk about a slob. There were dirty dishes everywhere. Bud Light cans were scattered about the counters and there was no kitchen table. And what the fuck was that sour smell? It was clear the garbage had not been out in days. My nose burned and my insides turned inside out. I fought back the bile that was rising in my throat. Ugh.

Slowly and very quietly I stepped out of the kitchen and onto an olive green carpet that led down a short hallway. The house was quiet but the farther I got down the hallway, I could hear a television. Then I saw a big opening coming up and I knew that had to be the living room. Approaching the living room, my heart started to beat faster. I was nervous. Sticking my head inside, I saw Silk—well, I saw his head. His back was facing me as he was sitting in a worn brown recliner.

I wasted no time creeping up behind him. I didn't make a sound so he must have sensed my presence. He jumped and turned around, but he was not quick enough because before he could say spit, I had my left arm wrapped around his throat with the Ruger to his skull.

"If I were you, I would sit very still," I whispered in his ear. I don't know why I whispered because I knew we were alone.

"Bitch, if you knew what best for you, you would get that gun from my head." I could not believe his audacity. Calling me a bitch like I was some common chick. Like I did not have heat cocked at the back of his brain.

"Nah, nigga, if you knew what was best for you, you wouldn't call me a bitch." I tapped him on the back of the head with the gun to remind him it was there. "Now where is Felicia? And don't lie to me."

"How da fuck should I know where dat hoe at?"

"Look, nigga." I pressed the Ruger to his temple. "Don't fuck wit' me because I will put one of these bullets in your head. Now just tell me where Imani is so I can get her back."

"Who da fuck is Imani?" he asked. He actually sounded like he was clueless as to the question. But I was not ready to believe him yet.

"My niece, motherfucker!" I yelled. "Felicia, that bitch you messin' with, she took my niece. And I want her back before dead bodies start piling up," I threatened, and I was ready to make good on that threat.

"I ain't got shit to do with that. You need to call that bitch. I don't kidnap kids and shit." For some reason I believed him. I just still could not believe that bitch would come up with something like this. Not all by herself. After I was done with her, she would hate the day she ever decided to fuck with my family.

Now there was the question about Hood. I was more than sure

that Silk knew what had happened to him. He was sitting in the recliner eyeballing me. I could tell he was wondering when I would bring Hood up. He also had killing me up his sleeve. I could tell his mind was racing trying to figure out his next move to take me down. But I was staring at him watching his every move and not once did I blink.

"Where Hood at? And I urge you not to fuck wit' me."

"Ha, ha, ha, ha." He started laughing. This nigga was psycho, he almost looked like the Joker. His evil-ass grin was that wide minus the makeup. "I knew you were going to ask me that. Actually I could not wait. I hated that nigga from the first time I met him." He stopped laughing and whipped the grin off his face. "How about you tell me where you think he at?"

I swallowed hard. That question caught me off guard. I could not believe he had the nerve to request that. Without warning, I took my Ruger and smacked him across the jaw with it. Blood flew out of his mouth and some down his throat; he coughed long and hard to keep from choking on it. I stood back and watched him catch his breath.

"Fuck you, bitch," he gurgled, his mouth still full of blood.

"No, fuck you, Silk. Now tell me where my husband at. Today is really not the day to be fucking wit' me."

"He dead, bitch. Nigga got just what he deserved. Yeah, he killed both of my partners, Dontae and Rico." My eyes grew wide at the mention of Rico. How did he know about Rico? "Yeah, that nigga bragged 'bout killin' my nigga Rico. Over yo stank ass. So you wanna know where he at? Find the closet, fucking dirt spot bitch..." He spat. I shot him in the knee, then took my gun and smacked him across the other side of his face. He screamed in agony for a good five minutes. I stood there and watched him. I couldn't kill him yet. I needed to find Felicia. And I needed him to tell me. Besides, something told me he was lying, Hood was not dead. If he was, I was sure I would know it in my heart. This nigga was lying, he was not the man in charge; Monty was.

"Look, I'm through fucking playing wit' yo ass. Tell me where

Felicia at. She yo bitch so I know you know where she be kickin' it at."

"I ain't tellin' you shit. So why don't you shoot me and get the fuck out." Talk about stubborn, this nigga was it. He sittin' in that recliner bleeding from the knee and mouth still tryna get smart. How he gone order me to kill him then put me out? Ha, he had some nerve, but it was time he really realized who was in charge. Clearly he had no real idea what I was capable of. Me putting a bullet in him was the least of his worries. I could think of something a whole lot more sinister and painful. He did not want to fuck with me.

"You know, Silk, I have given you ample chances and been very nice to you. But you continue to test my patience. Now I told you when I first got here that Felicia has my niece and I want her back." A tear slid down my face. I was getting emotional.

"So here is what I'ma do for you to help you out." I went inside my back pocket and pulled out a hunting knife that belonged to Hood. Hood was not a hunter, but he was a killer and sometimes he used different tools to finish the job. This hunting knife happened to be one of them. I was prepared to share it with Silk to get what I wanted.

I pointed the knife in his direction so that he could get a good look at. "If you do not tell me where I can find Felicia. . . ." I surveyed the knife myself. I could only imagine the damage it would do. And I knew that Silk was no stranger to knives with that cut he had running down the side of his face. I continued my proposition. "If you don't tell me where Felicia is, I'm going to take this knife and chop your dick OFF!" I screamed like a mad woman. "But I'm not going to take time to pull your pants down to do it the proper way. Nooo. . . ." I shook my head from side to side. "No, I'm going to take this knife and stab your dick with it and once it's in there really good, I'm going to pull it out then cut through your pants until I get to your pelvis area. Then I'm going to cut it off from your balls and put it in your MOUTH!" His facial expression was blank. So I made up my mind to show him I had no more time to waste.

I headed toward him with the knife in position to hit my mark. Right before I made the landing, Silk screamed. "Wait, wait, I'll tell you." Just like that he read off the address to me. As fast as he said it without stuttering, I knew he was not lying.

"See, that wasn't that hard now, was it. And guess what, for that you get to live." The look on his face was pure relief. He started to breathe again. I could see his shirt moving because for a minute it had stopped. I guess he was so nervous about me cutting off his manhood that he froze. I turned around as if to walk away and just like I thought, I felt Silk trying to move. I turned back to him in record time.

"Singing you a lullaby, bitch," I said, then put two bullets right between his eyes. You see, I knew he would try that. Did he really think I would walk away from there with him alive? Dummy. It just felt good to fuck with him to make him believe that he had a chance to live so that he could possibly kill me. Hilarious. Too bad I didn't have time to laugh. Others had death waiting on them.

Chapter 27

Breaking into Felicia's spot seemed to be risky once I saw her building. I knew it was some condos because Silk had said condo 356. I had just assumed it was made like some outside apartments. However, it turned out they were located inside the building. I had to go in then use the elevator. There were no back doors, only balconies, so I had one way to get in unless I wanted to climb up three flights. There was no way I risking falling trying to get up some tricky-ass balcony plus risk being seen by some nosy neighbor. Instead I decided on using the old credit card break-in trick. That was risky, too. Not being able to see inside the condo I had no clear vision of where she was at inside. Or if she was inside at all, because I had no idea what she was riding in. Some cars were inside the garages and some were sitting out on the street but I was clueless. The credit card was my only real hope of getting inside, so I went with what I knew. My heart pounded as I slid the card in and, as quietly as possible, I worked it and prayed that I didn't mess this up. I had to get the upper hand on her and, more important, I did not want Imani to get caught up in whatever jumped off.

Finally, the lock snapped open and I was inside the front door that led me into a hallway. The condo was quiet; I didn't even hear a television going. I was relieved that I had made it inside undetected but worried that they had run off. Down the hall to the right, I peeked inside the living room. I looked around and noticed that Felicia had the place decorated really nice. Coming from the Brewster-Douglass in that rat hole apartment she had been raised in, I knew she was doing better now. She had a bunch of brothers and sisters and they never had shit growing up. That's part of the reason she turned into a hoe so young. On an end table next to her loveseat there was a picture with her and Charlene at the club, of course.

I had not seen one glimpse of Charlene since I killed her and I must admit I didn't miss that selfish hoe. Felicia pulled me from my thoughts when she yelled out, "Silk, is that you babe?" I guess she had heard me come in. I was startled for just a second. The space was open—there was no place to hide—but even before I could, she was standing in the living room.

Shock graced her face: She was speechless for just a moment. I pointed the Smith & Wesson with the silencer attached at her.

"How did you get in here?" was the first question out of her mouth. I should have shot her ass for that.

"Really, bitch." I thought she had some nerve. Games were something I was not willing to play with her. "Is that all you have to say to me? Here is a question for you. Where is Imani?"

Instead of answering me, she threw her left hand on her hip. "Mya, as usual you barking up the wrong fuckin' tree. But I'ma give you some fucking advice. Get the fuck out. 'Cause I ain't got shit you want up in here."

"You gone advise me? Bitch, give me my niece before I blow your fucking head off. How about that, hoe." I pointed the gun from her abdomen to her head.

"You know what, go ahead and hang around if you want. Silk gone be here any minute and when he gets here he gone fuck you up. Think you the shit just 'cause you married to Hood. Hmmph." She sighed then rolled her eyes. This chick was off the chain with a backbone.

"So that's what you think? You think Silk gone ride in here on a white horse and save you. Well, bitch, I got news for you, the only time you gone ever see Silk again is when you meet his scarface-lookin' ass in hell. 'Cause I just murked that nigga 'bout an hour ago. How you think I found your little hiding spot? That nigga told me. Funny thing is that busta was talkin' cash shit just like you doing now." I started laughing as tears started trickling down her face. Emotional pain was a motherfucker. But she had not seen nothing yet.

"Now what you got to say? Do you wanna run that fucking trap of yours some more? Or you ready to give me my fucking niece back," I yelled. "Who kidnaps a fucking kid, Felicia? What type of person are you?"

"Fuck you, Mya, you ain't shit. I know what you did to Charlene. I know you killed her. Your ass walks around like you so fucking perfect and better than somebody else. But you not. You came from the Brewster just like us. Charlene was my best friend, my only friend." She cried. "She was the only person who cared about me and you took that away from me. And I have hated you for it for the last two years. That is why I sent my li'l cousin Anthony after your sister, Monica.

"He was supposed to hook up with her, get her alone, then kill her. But no, he had to go and start liking her, so my plan bombed. Shit." She stomped her feet like she had really lucked out. "But still I did not give up. Like my mom always say, there is more than one way to skin a cat." She was crazy. I could not believe my ears. This simpleminded bitch had planned to have my sister murdered. All because she mad at me for killing her so-called best friend. Anthony had been a setup plan all along. I cried inside. Was there anyone we could trust? Everyone that had come into our life seemed to have an agenda. I knew that Anthony was no good for Monica and to think she had no idea that he came into her life to end it. Thank God he fell first or I would be mourning her.

All because Felicia wanted to get some revenge on me. Wow. Money had gone to this bitch's head. She had gotten a little money, which had in turn gave her some confidence. Now she thought she could step to me. She had life messed up. And one thing I knew for sure: She was not about this life.

"Felicia, you weak. You a weak-ass bitch who can't fight your own battles. How you gone send a nigga to kill my sister?" I chuckle. "You know what, though? It don't even matter 'cause you played yourself."

"No, I didn't play myself, your sister got lucky." Suddenly she charged at me without warning. But my defenses are always up, so I clotheslined her with the butt of the gun. When she fell I tucked the gun in my waistband then I got on top of her and punched her in the face about three times. At first she wiggled and tried to fight back, but on the third punch she gave up and lay still. I had knocked the fight out of her at least for a minute.

"Kill me now if you want, but you still won't find Imani. So go ahead!" she screamed.

"Felicia, your whole plan had holes in it so just give it up. I also know about that fucking Monty you all been bowing down to. Tell me where to find him," I yelled in her face, still sitting on top of her.

By now her emotions had full control; she was crying and wiggling trying to free herself. But there was no chance in hell that I was letting her go. "Stop moving, Felicia, and tell me how to find Monty. It's over. All this bullshit ends tonight. Now where is he?"

"I will gladly tell you 'cause he gone kill you anyway," she said through snot and tears. She freely gave me the location. I could only hope she was telling the truth. I was sick of her crying ass. Now I needed Imani.

"Felicia, I know you mad at me about Charlene, but that shit is in the past. It has nothing to do wit' Imani. It is between us. Imani is a baby. Now where is she?" I asked as kindly as I knew because this would be her last chance. This was her chance to be a grownup.

But clearly Felicia was not ready for the grownup role in her life; instead she started laughing and her words cut me deep.

"She dead and buried, bitch. You got that, dead." She continued to laugh.

I smacked the smile off her face with my gun, then I forced her to open her mouth wide. She wanted to fuck with me about my niece. She wanted to be about this life. Well, I had her ticket to get her ass through the front gate. After forcing my Smith & Wesson down the back of her throat as far as I could fit it, I pulled the trigger, and with her eyes wide open I watched as Felicia's brains spilled all over her brand new white carpet.

To be honest, it brought me no joy. I was sick with hurt. I climbed off her and rested my back against the wall leading into her living room and cried. In less than two hours I had killed two people and still had not found Imani or Hood. The only answers I had received about them both was that they were dead. How could I tell my sister that I could not find her baby? The news would kill her. My mission was still not complete. I had to find Imani. With all my strength tied up in my pain, I tried to balance myself so that I could leave.

As I stood, I heard a toddler cry out. I was sure of it. The cry was low at first, then loud. I made my way down the hall then turned left, where I raced up some stairs. As soon as I snatched the first door open to my right I saw Imani was standing there. From the look of it, she had climbed out of the bed and was trying to turn the doorknob to open the door. Unsuccessful, she had cried for someone to open it for her. Seeing my face, she reached for me to pick her up, trying to call me Tee Tee. I hugged her so tight, I never wanted to let her go. And again I cried.

I took Imani straight to Monica. When I walked in the door with her, Monica looked as though she would pass out. We never discussed how I had found her. There was no need. We all agreed to tell the cops that we found her at a vacant house where an unknown caller told us she would be. Then we all sat around for a minute and cried and fussed over Imani but we knew she was fine. Felicia had done no harm to her. When I was in Felicia's room, I had seen that she had bags packed. Even a toddler suitcase was on the bed. It looked as though she was planning to run away with Imani. Sick bitch.

After making sure Ma, Monica, and Imani were all right, I told them I had to go. I needed to find Hood. My next stop was to visit Monty. Monica tried to talk me out of going anywhere. They just wanted me to stay, but they knew I had to go. Back inside the Bentley I reloaded my Ruger and Smith & Wesson. I had to make sure they were ready to go. I suited up with my heat and stabbed out. On the ride Rochelle crossed my mind. I had not spoken with her since that morning so I called her cell. It went straight to voice mail.

I then called the salon; she is always there, it is like her second home. Pam answered and told me that she had left earlier and had not returned. Since it was late, I told Pam to go ahead and lock up for the night. I thought it unusual that Rochelle never returned, but something may have come up with Tiny. That is the only time she ever took off. In another attempt to reach her before I reached my destination, I dialed her number again. Once again it went straight to voice mail. This time I decided to leave her a voice mail. Because as tough as I was, I knew I was walking into trouble's arms. I knew whoever this Monty was, he was no joke and would without a second thought kill me. So I wanted to leave a message for my friend just in case this was her last time hearing my voice. But don't get it twisted, I had my game face on and I was not going down without a fight. Hood was my husband and he meant the world to me. And Monty owed me the answer to where he was and I was willing to lay my life down and die for that answer.

Chapter 28

With the help of my GPS it took me two hours to find the spot where Monty was supposed to be keeping his ass hidden out at. Not to mention it was late as hell. My eyes were starting to feel a little heavy, but I was still in control. Nothing would keep me from this mission tonight. The area was secluded and surrounded by a lot of tall grass. It was dark except for the lights on the rusty building that I was hoping to find him in. The building looked like an old factory and had to be at least a hundred years old. Was this the best spot they could find? It was leaning so much to the left, I was sure it would cave at any given moment. The thought of the building caving in with me inside made me feel some type of way. I quickly brushed it off, though, because I had to get inside. As soon as I was in closer eyesight of the building, I hit my lights. I didn't want to be noticed before I was ready to make my move. I was sure he had bodyguards watching out for him. A pussy-ass nigga always ran with a big dude to protect his so-called hard ass. Hmmph, that thought had me shaking my head.

When I got out of the car, I stayed low in the tall grass while getting a good look at my surroundings. But I had to get closer to see the entrance part of the shack. I'm sure Hood had been to this spot at least once. As I got closer, I saw three vehicles that I had not seen before. There was a black Jaguar, a beat-up red Honda, and a tan Dodge pickup truck.

I was well aware that I could possibly be walking into a lynch mob without no chance at all of survival. I closed my eyes and took a deep breath. When my eyes closed, I saw the warm sun shining on my face with the wind blowing. I looked over and saw Monica, Imani, Ma, Dad, and Li'l Bo all standing there with me smiling. A smile spread across my lips as a tear slid down my face, then the sun was gone. I had a job to do, because Hood was missing from that picture. Inside, the place reeked of old metal, dust, and weed. The smell snatched at my stomach. I tried to hold it but vomit spewed from my mouth without any self-control. I wiped my mouth with the back of my hand. I tried to stand back up even though the smell was overwhelming. As I took a light step, I heard something fall onto the concrete. It sounded like a wrench butting heads with the wet pavement. I was not sure what it was, but it was hard metal.

I stood still for a moment. My heart was pounding so fast, I thought I could hear it. All of a sudden something heavy came down on my back, I think.

My eyes scanned the ceiling. I was sure I was hallucinating: The last thing I remember was the weight of the world coming down on top of me. I felt as if my eyes were opened wide, but the ceiling and the lights hanging from the ceiling seemed dim. I wanted to physically stretch my eyes open myself but neither of my arms were working. I was confused until I realized I was lying on my back. I tried to kick my legs for freedom but it felt as if I was trying to kick with tons of bricks. I panicked. Trying to survey my surroundings, I saw this guy standing over me. I moved my eyes downward; I saw that I was tied to a bed. Anxiety set in: I needed to think. I moved my head left to right. Suddenly, I remembered where I was. But the guy is unfamiliar. I remembered why I was here and then Monty came to mind. My voice sounded groggy when I spoke.

"Who the fuck are you? Untie me from this filthy bed!" I

managed to scream. The short, stout guy just looked at me with a blank expression and left the room. At least that was what it appeared to be. This room did not look as rusty as it did from the outside. I heard the unknown guy yell for Monty. I would finally see who this asshole was. Feeling scared but eager, I tried to sit up. I could not wait to be face to face with him, even though I was aware that being in this position, I had no control over the situation.

"Damn it!" I hit my head against the bed, angry at myself. How had I ended up tied to this bed? I would be killed before I could find out anything about Hood. No one was coming to help me because I had told no one exactly where I was going. "Shit!" I screamed again. My independence had finally put me in the wrong position, but I could not cry. I needed to see what was in store. So I lay still and waited for fate to come.

Then this guy who I assumed was Monty stepped into the room, and I knew I had to be dreaming. Had my nightmares come true? I froze, my breathing stopped, my fear was so strong I closed my eyes tight. Maybe if I kept them closed long and hard enough I would wake up from this nightmare. I would be home in bed and Hood would be calling my name. I prayed but seconds passed, then minutes, and nothing. I was still lying in the same position. The rhythm of my heart was threatening to come through my chest. Slowly I opened my eyes up to face him. I had no other choice.

This time when I opened my eyes, the blurry vision had cleared up. My eyesight was back one hundred percent. I gazed at this so-called Monty in horror.

"Shocked, right, bitch? Well, this ain't a dream and I ain't Luscious," he informed me with a grin, holding a blunt in his hand. "No, I'm his twin brother, Monty." Suddenly everything was clear. We had all been set up. Two years after Luscious's murder and the nightmare still was not over. That fucking Luscious would not rest until I was dead. A twin? I would have never imagined this.

"So you have been behind all this shit? You help set it up for my niece Imani to be kidnapped? You helped that bitch Felicia plan to set up my sister?" My nerves had slowed and I got pissed. I wanted answers.

"Hold up, sweetheart. I don't know shit about nobody named Imani being kidnapped. I don't harm kids. Okay? Let's get that shit straight. As for that sneaky hoe bitch Felicia, I ain't had shit to do wit' her besides maybe banging her couple of times." He started laughing, then hit his blunt. "Nah, that shit ain't have nothing to do wit' Monty. Anthony punk ass, all he was supposed to do was to rob one of Hood li'l spots. Just to fuck wit' him and throw him off. But his punk ass couldn't even do that without gettin' murked. These niggas be dumb." He hit his blunt again and walked closer to the bed.

I could not believe Anthony's ass. He had tried to come at my family from both sides, working for Felicia and Monty. I knew he was trouble. Like always, I was a good judge of character. I tried to move again. I wanted to be released. "Where the fuck is Hood, bitch? Tell me what did you do with him. You already killed Pablo and Rob. Now where my husband at?" I barked as tears escaped my eyes. I yanked hard, but the ropes on my wrist were too tight.

"What's the matter, is the ropes too tight?" He had the nerve to grin. For the first time I realized that his teeth were not real. They were too white and straight. He walked over to the bed and rubbed his hands across my thighs. I saw the lust in his eyes. "Damn, you fine, li'l momma. That shit too damn bad."

"Fuck you, dick face, and keep your stubby-ass hands off me!" I spat with pure disgust. He was identical to Luscious; he just weighed about thirty pounds more.

Instead of being offended, he started to laugh a deep, throaty laugh. It almost sounded as if he was clogged from a cold. "You know this setup was pretty much easy because I knew you would come for Hood. From what I hear, you already bodied two people tonight just to get to me." That bit of information was a surprise to my ears. How did he find out so quick I had killed Silk and Felicia?

"See, the one thing I learned about you from checking your past was that you are a gangsta bitch to the fullest." After he complimented me, he started to clap his hands together, holding the still-lit blunt between his closed lips. Finally he stopped and stepped back from the bed. "You deserve a round of applause. Had it not been for this situation, you coulda been my main bottom bitch."

"Nigga, don't flatter yourself," I spat. "The only thing you could ever get from me is a bullet, bitch." I hoped I had made that clear. His punk ass had some nerve.

I could not believe how creepy Monty was. I started to open my mouth again, but then I heard some labored moaning. The kind of moans that a person makes when they are in pain. The sound was coming from the left of me. I looked at Monty, who smiled but said nothing. I slowly turned my head in that direction. It was Rochelle. Her clothes were ripped and she was lying in a pool of blood.

A sigh escaped my throat. It felt as though I had swallowed a ball the size of an egg, but it was just a huge knot. I tried my best to breathe. Rochelle looked close to death. Why had he done this to her? She was innocent. I had done everything possible to keep her out of this. She had nothing to do with Luscious's death.

"Rochelle," I called her name. "Rochelle," I tried again. I was sick with hurt. She did not deserve this. More important, she had Tiny who needed her. Her body lay still and she had stopped moaning. I was sure she was unconscious now. Who knows how long she had been here with this monster. Now I knew why she never came back to the salon or answered her phone. She had been kidnapped, too. All because of me. Everyone was suffering in some way because of me and what I had done.

Keeping my eyes on Rochelle, I asked him, "What did you do to her?" My voice was calm and my body numb from shock.

"Oh, don't worry yo pretty li'l head about her, she just faking. Shit, I just did to her what I do to all my hoes when I fuck 'em."

The blood in my veins thickened. Was this asshole saying that he had raped my friend? My eyes burned so bad they had to be bloodshot red. This motherfucker had tried it. He was right, I was a gangsta bitch. And not even he could control what I would do.

"Don't be mad, Ma. Your turn is coming, too. I been waiting to kill you for two years. Don't worry, you will enjoy it just like me. I promise."

I turned to face him with venom coming from my tongue. I wanted to make myself very clear, so I hoped he was listening. "Listen up and listen good." I swallowed. "You better take whatever weapon you got and kill me. Because if I get the chance, you a dead motherfucker. You got that, bitch!" I spat without blinking an eye. "You done fucked with the wrong female."

"That I can believe." He was licking his lips and looking at me like I was a T-bone steak on display. He sat down on the bed. He slowly reached for the button on my jeans and I screamed for him to get his hands off. But a calm come over me when I see Big Nick creeping up. He put the nine-millimeter Glock to the back of Monty's head. Monty froze with wide eyes like the bitch he was.

"One wrong move and the last thing you will see is darkness," Big Nick warned in no uncertain terms. Monty knew he meant business.

"I want you to untie those ropes from around her arms. And slow..." He pushed Monty's head with the gun. I looked from Monty to Big Nick with wondering eyes. With a few light tugs, the ropes fell off. Slapping Monty in the face as hard as I could, I flew into Big Nick's arms. Big Nick never took the nine off Monty. I quickly sprang back to the matter at hand. We had no time to waste and could not lose control of the situation.

Big Nick threw me a Ruger that I instantly knew was mine. He must have found it while making his way inside. I knew without question that stout guy from earlier had met his maker. I held the Ruger to Monty's head and thanked Big Nick for coming while he tied Monty up. We questioned Monty about Hood but he refused to give us any information. Even after Big Nick punched him in the face about five times with the butt of his nine-millimeter. The pain caused him to temporarily black out.

"Fuck this shit, ain't no use, this place is big. I'ma take a look around to see if I can find anything." Big Nick wiped the blood that had landed on his hands and clothes while he beat Monty onto the bedspread.

"Okay, yeah, go ahead and look around, but hurry, we got to get Rochelle to the hospital." I wiped at the snot and tears that were running down my face. I made my way over to Rochelle, who was now lying on a beat-up couch. She looked totally different. Both of her eyes were swollen. There were bruises on her face, arms, and hands, and blood was all over her clothes. I looked at her finger-nails and saw blood. I could tell she had put up a good fight. I put my face to her chest and cried. I could feel her heart beating so I knew she was still alive. Monty would pay for all that he had done at this point. I started to believe that I would never find out what happened to Hood. All of this and I still had no answers.

Turning around and looking at the bed, I saw there was no Monty. I stood just in time. That slick motherfucker had got the ropes off. I guess I should not have been surprised: They were his ropes. It would be only natural that his snake ass knew how to work them. But the one thing he did not have was a piece. I guess he thought being in his own spot would give him the upper hand. He had been too stupid to bring one along with him when his chubby bodyguard had alerted him that I was awake. The ball was still in my court and I did not hesitate.

I pointed the Ruger at him. He stood still, but I walked toward him and kicked him in the balls so hard that he fell to his knees. Blood was still dripping from his mouth from the beating that Big Nick put on him. He erupted with laughter. Evil people always had pride.

"It don't matter that you have that gun, bitch." He wiped at the blood. "You still gone be murked for what you did to my brother. There is a lot more people like me out there. The stakes will only get higher after tonight." I guess this was supposed to be a threat on my life. But who gave a fuck? She who had the mother-fucking gun ruled.

"Fuck your brother. Who cares what happened to him? That nigga wasn't shit. That's why I kill that nigga over and over in my dreams and love every minute of it." I grinned.

Out of the blue Monty charged at me, but I released the Ruger and hit him in the right shoulder. He fell back into the bed. As soon as he hit the sheets, he started cursing me out and calling me bitch. Like those words could hurt me of all people. I was tired of this charade. I would show and tell.

Taking the butt of the Ruger, I rushed over to him and I hit him in the jaw three times. Again blood flew out of his mouth, then a tooth. I realized his teeth were real, but ugly as fuck. Now that I think about it, there were some differences in him and Luscious. Monty was the ugly version.

"What happened to Hood? Just tell me!"

"He dea—" Before he could finish his word, I hit him in the same jaw with the Ruger. This time I felt his jaw crack. That jaw had finally had it; it could not take another blow.

"Where the fuck is Hood!" I screamed again desperately. I knew he was not going to tell me.

He was barely able to talk, but he still tried to brag about Hood's ill fate. "He dead just like you gone be soon. After I let my men beat him for days, I ordered them to throw his weak ass in a pit with my hungry bloodhound-eating pit bulls." He started laughing again. He was in so much pain, tears were forming in his eyes but still he laughed at me. "I guess I get the last laugh, huh, bitch."

Tears poured down my face. I was speechless as events from my past played in my mind. The first time Squeeze beat my mom, my first robbery, the first time I met Hood, Li'l Bo being killed, all the way to Monica killing Luscious. After all of that, I tried to live my life right, even though I still struggled with the hurt of losing Li'l Bo and my sister having to kill Luscious to save my life. I tried to live right and I had even tried to force it on Hood. All the while hurt and pain was still busting down doors and enemy lines just to get to me. It seemed to find me and my beloved family no matter what. For the first time in my life I questioned if my sweetest revenge was worth it.

Monty broke my thoughts and helped me answer my most important question.

"Go ahead and kill me, bitch, because I have been dead for a long motherfucking time. And I will meet your soul in hell." Monty's pain was not my sorrow.

"With pleasure." I bucked my Ruger and didn't stop until it was empty. Yes, my sweetest revenge was worth it. Shit like Monty, Luscious, or Squeeze don't deserve to roam the earth. No, this world was better off without them.

Shaking with grief over my husband, I dropped the Ruger to the floor and cried from my soul.

"It's okay, baby girl; you did what you had to do." There was only one person who called me that name besides my dad. It had been a long time since he called me that, though he had stopped after he heard Dad call me that. I turned and there stood Hood. I ran into his arms and I hugged him so tight that he yelped out in pain.

Monty had not lied about beating him, he was beat up pretty bad. Without wasting any more time, Big Nick grabbed Rochelle, and I helped Hood to the car. Then we sped straight to the hospital.

Chapter 29

Six Months Later

Six months later and I was still sitting around daily counting my blessings. Life was slowly but surely coming back to normal. Turns out that it was Ma who had called up Big Nick and told him I needed help. She had declared that she would not lose another child to the streets, so she stepped up and went out on a limb. Sharing all the information that Dad had told her about Monty, they were able to connect the dots. After hanging up with her, Big Nick had got on the phone and made two phone calls. One was to his ear connection to the street and then another to get a trace on Monty's hideout.

See, Big Nick was from the old streets, which meant he had eyes and ears that neither I nor Hood would ever have. I guess you can say he had paid his dues or, as Dad would say, he "paid the cost to be the boss." Either way, I owed him big for saving my life as well as my husband. I was in his debt. With his help we had gotten Rochelle and Hood to the hospital in time. They had both sustained terrible beatings. Hood's rib cage had been severely cracked but not broken.

Rochelle, on the other hand, had been beaten so badly that she suffered a miscarriage. Yeah, she had been pregnant with Dontae's baby. But she had had no idea. According to records, she was in early stages, not yet two months. Because of the miscarriage she had lost a lot of blood. So much that the doctor said if we had not gotten her to them when we did that she would have died. That statement alone made my heart beat a whole lot different. I was happy to find out that she had not been raped, though. The doctors said there was no sign of rape, and when Rochelle woke up the next day, she confirmed it. Rochelle said that the guy that had kidnapped her tried to rape her but she fought him so long and hard he gave up. Said he told Monty, "I don't wanna fuck that bitch, she crazy." He then took his bloody nose and scratched-up face, and limped away holding his balls. She said that Monty beat on her for a while after that until she blacked out. When she woke up, she was in the hospital. I was sick with guilt for days. I would not eat and I quickly lost ten pounds. My ma came to me and pulled me back to life. Normally, I gave her the pep talk, but therapy was helping her a lot. Now she was able to be strong for me.

Things were getting better every day. Hood and Rochelle were released from the hospital months ago and everybody's lives seemed to be falling into step. Rochelle had hooked back up with Todd and was engaged to be married. She had finally admitted she was in love with him all along. His constant commitment scared her. After losing Li'l Lo she was afraid of falling in love again. I was really happy for them, and Ms. Wynita was over the hills that the Lord had finally answered her prayers.

Hood was also getting his shit together. As soon as he was able to walk, and I guess I should say run, again he got on the phone and called up one of his old guys that had moved to Miami a couple years back. He went by Walt on the streets, and the streets knew not to fuck with Walt. Walt was like six foot six and weighed about two seventy-five. To the ladies he was a teddy bear, but the niggas knew not to cross him. Hood said that Walt would be the perfect man to take over his operation. Walt took the offer with pleasure and flew out to Detroit right away. Hood worked with him for about two months setting up connects and letting everyone know that Walt was the new man.

Before officially letting the reins go, Hood suggested that we all take a trip to Disneyland. Everybody happily agreed. With no hesitation, our whole family hopped on a plane headed to California. We even brought Rochelle, Todd, Tiny, and Ms. Wynita along. It was going down, we had planned five fun-packed days in the sun.

And what can I say? When we laid eyes on Disneyland, it was what we all had imagined and more. I shed a few tears for the fact Li'l Bo and Dad were not there. But I would not let that spoil my trip; besides, we would be getting word any day now about Dad's possible parole. We didn't want to get our hopes up too high only to be let down. But Hood was paying the attorney a lot of fucking money, so we stayed positive.

We were down to the last day of the trip; we had seen and done so much already until exhaustion crept up on us. But that didn't stop nothing. We still wanted to see all we possibly could before leaving. This day was different, though, because the night before Rochelle, Todd, Monica, Hood, and I had partied. It was Monica's birthday, plus she had graduated a month before. With all the craziness we had not celebrated the way we wanted to. So we found a club, set up VIP for us only, and kicked it. We popped bottles till like four in the morning. Talk about turn up! We did and in somebody else's city. Detroit was in the house. By the time Hood and I got back to our room. we were out like a light, but only for a little while. No sooner than my head hit the pillow, Ma was ringing the room.

"Hello," I said in a morning groggy tone.

"Look, I know y'all got it in last night, but wake up."

"But Ma, I'm tired, we both tired. Besides it's early," I complained. But this was Marisa and I knew she would not let it go. And if we didn't listen to her, Ms. Wynita would be next, and she would be ten times worse.

"Girl, it ain't early, it twelve o'clock and this is the last day. So hop to it and meet us downstairs."

I rolled over and looked at the clock. It was 12:01 p.m. Shit, it felt like I had been asleep for twenty damn minutes, not eight hours. "Okay." I gave in, then hung up.

"Hood, babe," I said, looking in his direction. He turned over and wrapped himself tighter in the covers. "Come on, babe, get up, that was Ma. You know she gone be beating on this door next."

"Damn, Mya, I just laid down." He tried to use the same excuse on me that I gave to Ma.

I started laughing. "Babe, get up, it's twelve. We been asleep." I told him the time just like Ma had informed me.

"Well, I must still be drunk. That Don Julio got me fucked up." He lifted his head a little, smiled, and then put his face back on his pillow. "I ain't gone make it. But look, you go ahead and I'll be down in about two hours. I promise," he begged. "Tell Ma Marisa I'm sick." He laughed.

"A'ight, but you better come down." I threw the covers back and headed for the shower. I felt energized afterwards. I was dressed just in time for Monica to knock on our door. I grabbed my Prada shades, slid them on, and headed out. Downstairs everyone was waiting to hit it. Once outside, I realized I had left my cell phone. I had to keep my cell phone on me just in case Pam or Trina called. I left them in charge of the salon until I got back. I knew they could handle it because they knew how everything worked. But I assured them I would always be available when they called. It would be just my luck that they called when I left my cell. I used Monica's phone to call Hood in the room on his cell but got no answer. Damn, I had no choice but to go get it.

After convincing Ma I would be back, I started back to the hotel. As I got on the elevator Rochelle and Todd approached.

"Wait a minute, where the hell y'all going." I smiled. They were like kids in love, all over each other.

"Look, we trying to spend some alone time before we leave this big ass beautiful hotel. I haven't been able to pry Tiny off. Shit, we 'bout to break that damn bed in." Rochelle laughed and Todd grabbed her into a hug and they kissed.

"Damn, wit' all that, I guess y'all do need some alone time. 'Cause all that unnecessary slobbering each other down is way too much for my eyesight," I joked, then hit the button to take us up to the tenth floor where our suites were. Hood had paid for the entire trip and of course he made sure we all had the best.

Halfway through our ride, the elevator chimed to make a stop. I looked at a kissing Rochelle and Todd. "Y'all gone have to chill out. We about to have company on this ride," I joked again.

"Shit, they can join the show." Rochelle smiled then rubbed Todd's head and he grabbed her booty tight. I shook my head at them. They were funny.

The elevator settled so that the doors could open. With a smile spread across my face, I watched the doors slide back. I was not ready for what I saw. A guy was standing in the hall with a gun pointed directly at me, his eyes glued only on me. His lips moved and as the words "Checkmate, bitch!" rolled off his tongue, I heard the bullet leave the chamber.

The heaviness of Todd's body knocked me to the back wall of the elevator. Then I heard two more gunshots. The shooter seemed to stand still with an unexpected look of shock pouring from his face. As I watched a bullet rip through the back of his spine, his eyes never left mine. Then before his body could hit the ground, another bullet hit him in the back of his head and it split like a melon. I watched his body fall and I saw Hood standing there.

At that same moment, Todd's body hit the floor and I was covered in his blood. I looked from Todd's motionless body to the blood I was covered in and then over to Rochelle. I started to shake violently.

Rochelle fell to the floor with Todd and slowly lifted him into her lap. She screamed, "No, No, No!" She rocked back and forward with him as her cries rang in my ears like bullets. Monty's threats came back to haunt my mind. He told me the chances of me being killed were going to get higher after his death. With all this death on my hands, would my sweetest revenge ever end?

HER SWEETEST REVENGE 2

Saundra

ABOUT THIS GUIDE

The questions that follow are included
to enhance your group's reading of this book.

Discussion Questions

1. Mya's nightmares about Luscious are constant. Is it possible the nightmares are from guilt or from fear of the dream becoming a reality?

2. Mya declared that she and Hood had more than enough money. Therefore she wanted him out of the game ASAP. Do you think it's selfish of her to demand this, knowing that was his way of life before they got married?

3. Mya was upset when she first met Anthony, mainly because she saw him coming out of the back of the condo. Was she overstepping her boundaries by scolding Monica or questioning her about the situation?

4. Rochelle dumps Todd, a guy who loved her and cared for her daughter, Tiny, only to turn to Dontae, a known pusher in the area. Is it possible she broke up with Todd because she felt guilty for being in love with someone other than Li'l Lo, whom she clearly missed?

5. With Rob being killed in New York on a deal set up through Rico, Dontae, and Silk, should Hood have been a little suspicious of them? Should he have questioned their character or true intentions?

6. After Felicia had been to the salon twice acting up being loud and disrespectful, was Mya out of place for finally losing her temper and lashing back out, including fighting?

7. Marisa admits to Monica and Mya that she was depressed and afraid her addiction might return. Will taking the step to reach out to her family for help make her fight harder to remain drug free? Or will she most likely cave under pressure, knowing the temporary comfort the drugs might bring?

8. Will Rochelle blame Mya for Todd's death? If so, will this incident threaten their friendship?

Don't miss the next installment—*Her Sweetest Revenge 3*! Available March 2016 wherever books and ebooks are sold.

Chapter 1

We stayed in California four weeks after the shooting and everything still felt like a bad dream that I could not wake up from. For three of those four weeks, Todd was on life support, hanging on to dear life for as long as he could.

His mother, Louise, had received the bad news of him being shot over the telephone and took the first flight out to California to be by her only son's side. Upon arriving, she had been distraught past comfort, yet determined to see Todd live. After weeks of watching him lie there hooked up to dozens of machines with no change and hearing the doctor deliver the same speech to her day after day, she finally accepted the fact that there was no hope of him ever recovering. So with a calm, blank stare on her face, she reached for the pen and silver clipboard the nurse held out to her. Her hands shook violently as she signed the paperwork that sealed Todd's fate. He was gone. Rochelle was devastated. She had spent days in the hospital chapel praying. For days she didn't eat anything and she only drank liquid at the threat of the doctor hospitalizing her if she didn't. I knew without a doubt that it was my fault. No one said it, but I knew.

It was shortly after Todd died that Rochelle demanded that I tell her the entire truth about Squeeze. She had been in and out of consciousness when Monty had kidnapped her and she had overheard Monty and me arguing. After putting two and two together, she'd figured out it was revenge for what I had done to Squeeze. But wanting to forget the entire situation she endured, she had never asked and I totally understood.

But once Todd was killed, that all changed and she wanted to know everything. She said she had to make sense of why every-thing had happened and why every man that she loved had been killed. I told her without any reluctance, even though I understood the risk. I owed her that much. Now she knew exactly how much blood I had on my hands, including Charlene's, one of our former close friends. Who, in my opinion, had committed the ultimate be-trayal—deceit. But only I looked like the monster.

Finally, after Todd's body was shipped back to Detroit and the funeral held, life was slowly moving on. A couple of weeks had passed since the burial and I was back to work at the salon. I had to do something to keep myself busy. I just wanted to forget that I was ultimately to blame for all of the bad shit that had happened. But that was easier said than done.

"Mya," Keisha, one of Rochelle's regulars, called my name and pulled me away from my private thoughts.

I was sewing in her new round of blond-colored Brazilian hair. She wore it long down her back in big locks. She had been bab-bling a mile a minute and I had not heard a word.

"Damn, you day dreaming? Or are your ears plugged?" She ac-cused with sarcasm in her tone.

"Oh, my bad. I was thinking about something for a minute. What's up? What did I miss?" I chuckled to play it off. There was no way she would understand my situation.

"I was just asking when do you think Rochelle comin' in? I tried to call her the other day just to see how she was doing. She didn't answer though."

I wanted to say *join the club* but I decided against it.

"Dang, what you don't like my work or somethin'?" I joked as I stuck the needle back in to start a new row. I had to compliment myself, it was flowing just right.

"Whatever," She laughed. "Real talk: I'm just worried about my girl. That's all."

I saw the concern on her face in the mirror. Honestly, I knew how she felt. I felt the same way times ten. But I had to assure her that all was good. Rochelle wouldn't want me to say otherwise.

"I know, but she good. She just gettin' a little rest, that's all."

I reassured her with a smile. Just as I pulled the needle all the way through the track, Hood walked in. I instantly knew something was up by the look on his face. What can I say, I know my man.

"What's up, Hood?" Keisha asked. Her younger brother, Drew, worked for the Height Squad.

"What's up?" He spoke to her while looking directly at me. He wanted to talk. It was written all over his face. "Hey babe, can I holla at you for a minute?" he finally said.

"Sure. Give me a second. I'll meet you in the back."

I always tried to remain professional or least I did my best. After pulling the needle completely out, I told Keisha I'd be right back.

"Ah, you straight," she said as she started scrolling through her Instagram pics.

As soon as I opened the door to the room that we used as a break room, I found Hood pacing back and forth. Yeah, something was definitely up. I took a quick, deep breath. Just in case I would have to ease it out slowly.

"What's wrong?" I braced myself but was still not prepared.

"It's Walt. He dead. Somebody rolled up on him at a red light on the block about an hour ago and pumped him full of bullets."

"You gotta be fuckin' kiddin' me." I was shocked. The dude had just started running the crew and already somebody put out a hit on him. What the fuck? The game was a bitch.

"What happened? Do you know who did it?"

"Word on the streets is that it was a hit from Florida. Niggas say he was into some people back in Florida for some big money and a murder."

"So what you gone do?" That was my new concern. I really didn't want him to get involved.

"I can't do shit about that. That was on him. His old baggage, he shoulda took care of that. He knew the rules. I hate that he even brought that shit here. He told me he was clean. But whatever, that's done."

The look on his face showed that he meant what he was saying. That was it. To be honest, I was relieved that he was not going to retaliate. Something told me that this was not it though, he had something else to drop on me.

"What is it, Hood? Tell me straight out. I got a weave to finish." I was agitated because I knew what was coming next.

Hood put both his hands on his head and rubbed them back and forth then sighed. "Well, as you already know, Walt didn't completely have the torch yet. I had planned to turn it over to him over the next couple of weeks. So technically, it's still mine. And the streets already buzzin' non-stop."

That I was not shocked about. These streets are monstrous twenty-four-seven, they stay waiting for the next move or come up.

I folded my arms across my chest and cleared my throat. "What's your point?"

I continued to play dumb. He would have to say it. I refused to let him off the hook easy.

"I have to take the streets now before a war gears up. These niggas ready to try to claim some shit. You already know I ain't havin' it. Besides, if I don't, dead bodies gone be all over the place, innocent people included. The words new territory makes these niggas buck."

As much as I hated to admit it, he was right. The Height Squad had to have their leader or Detroit would become a war zone for their spot. Niggas would fight for the trap houses and their territory, or at least territory they could try to take over. And addicts would do anything for their next hit, because if they couldn't cop they would trip out, too. Hood had no choice. These were the hard facts. As much as I wanted to fight him on this, I could not.

"I guess you gotta do what you gotta do."

I gave in as a single tear slid down my right cheek. My husband was back in the life that he seemed not to be able to escape. And his fate was ultimately mine. I wiped the tear away. There was no need for it.

"I gotta get back to Keisha."

I turned to leave, my heart in my stomach.

"Babe."

Hood reached out, took my hand and turned me towards him. He looked me deep in the eyes with nothing but love and sincerity.

"I'm sorry. But I promise you right here and right now that this is not going to be forever. I promise you that."

I so wanted to believe that. But was it true?

He kissed my forehead then my lips slowly before I turned and walked away.

Chapter 2

After Hood laid that news on me yesterday, I felt mentally exhausted. I went home, climbed into bed, and slept until morning. I wasn't depressed, just tired of all the things that kept coming at me. It felt like a never-ending circle. My body had concluded that sleep would be the best method of dealing with it and after waking up feeling fresh, I agreed. I brushed off my shoulders, pulled back my bedroom drapes, and said good morning to the sun that was shining beautifully outside. I jumped in my white Range Rover and pointed it in the direction of Rochelle's condo. It had been two full days since I had heard from her.

Pulling up to her condo I noticed that she had her Lexus parked outside along with her new sports Mercedes Benz truck she had copped right before our trip to California. Normally, she kept one of her cars in her connected two-car garage. I jumped out of the Range and headed up to the door and pressed the doorbell. Three rings later, there was no answer so I started to knock. She knew how much I hated to wait, as I was known to be impatient. As my fist went up for round two of knocking, the door swung open.

The solemn look on Rochelle's usually happy face clearly said that she didn't want to be bothered. She pulled her baby blue

Prada robe tighter around her body and asked, "Why didn't you call first?"

A slight frown crossed my face, because her question threw me off.

"Since when do I have to call first? And what took you so long to answer the door?"

I threw questions back at her as she wanted to be a grouch. Not waiting on her to give me an answer, I stepped around her and into the condo. I instantly stopped. She had all the drapes drawn tightly shut. It was so dark that I could barely see in front of me to take another step. I turned to Rochelle as she rubbed her hand through her hair.

"Look, I don't mean to be snapping on you, but I was just gettin' into a good sleep. And to be honest, I don't get that often lately," she admitted, and I felt guilty.

"Sorry, I just wanted to check on you. But why all the darkness? I mean I can't see shit." I scanned the darkness again. And the results were the same pure darkness. Without answering, Rochelle hit the switch and a light came on, brightening the room. Finally, I could see and relief swept over me. Looking around the room, I saw a blanket on the couch and an ashtray full of cigarette butts. It was obvious she had been sleeping and chain smoking. The smell of the smoke clouded my nostrils and filled my lungs at the same time. I coughed.

"Rochelle, what is going on?"

I was worried. I knew she had not been feeling well. But smoking packs of cigarettes back to back was not the answer. The look on her face showed her agitation just a little bit. She turned her head away from me.

"Nothing Mya, just trying to get some sleep and relax," she stated as she pulled her robe even tighter around her. The grip she had on it was deathly and I understood why. She had the AC on frost. She headed to the sofa with the blanket, plopped down, and wrapped herself up.

"Why do you have it so damn cold in here?" I managed to say, my teeth were clicking together from the cold.

"It helps me sleep better."

"Where is Tiny?"

I realized she was nowhere in sight. Tiny always came out of her room when Rochelle answered the door. I always joked that she was Rochelle's bodyguard.

"She's with Wynita. I'm supposed to pick her up later today. But I might let her spend one more night."

Rochelle had had a doctor's appointment scheduled the day before. I wanted to know if he had found anything wrong with her.

"What did the doctor say?"

"Nothin' much. According to him I just need some rest. And to be honest I agree and that's exactly what I'm trying to do."

Throwing the blanket back, she reached for her pack of Newports off the table. She lit a cigarette, took a drag, and relief instantly displayed across her face. Pushing her hair off her face, she looked at me and exhaled. A cloud of smoke rushed the air.

"But I should be back to work soon."

"Don't worry about that right now. I want you to get better first."

I smiled at her, but she didn't smile back. Instead, she took another drag from her cigarette and blew out another cloud of smoke. I almost felt like those clouds were accusing me of something. But I released that crazy thought as quickly as it had come.

Suddenly, I had a good idea. It had been a minute since we had been out to lunch together. Actually, it had been back before the California trip and that felt like a lifetime ago. Nothing had been normal since. Not that anything in my life ever was.

"How about we grab some lunch? I'm hungry as hell. I haven't had anything to eat since lunch time yesterday," I admitted. After Hood had laid that information on me, I'd completely lost my appetite and two pounds.

Blowing out more cigarette smoke and sitting forward on her couch, Rochelle put her cigarette out in the ashtray.

"Not today Mya. I just want to get back to sleep. But maybe some other time."

She wrapped herself back up in her blanket and lay down. I almost felt like she was kicking me out and I was running out of things to say. Feeling like shit about my best friend's grief, I told her bye and bounced.

After grabbing a quick bite for myself, I headed to the salon for the day. Leslie had a two-thirty appointment with me to get her hair done.

"What's up, boss lady," Pam spoke as I strolled through the door of my successful establishment.

As always, when I entered my salon I felt a bit of bliss. I was a proud business owner, because I had literally started from the bottom but now was here. I mean my life was not squeaky clean, as everybody is already aware, but I knew God was good and I had hope.

"Ain't nothin'. I'm good." I followed up. "Is everything running smoothly around here?" Since Rochelle had been off everyone's workload had increased. But we kicked butt as a team with no complaints.

"Yeah. I just booked a last-minute appointment for Fantasia Barrino. She's in town for a show and her stylist fell ill. And of course, we were referred as the hottest in town. Her bodyguard and her assistant will be bringing her by in about three hours."

"Is Trina ready?"

"Of course, she already knocked out her first three for the morning. She just stepped out to lunch and will be back in time. And she has three more scheduled for later tonight." Pam beamed.

"Alright that's what's up." I smiled as well.

The news made me happy, not only because Fantasia was coming, but because in the last six months our celebrity clientele, which included K-Michelle and CoCo from SWV to name a few, had increased through referral. My girls Pam and Trina were always on top of their game. Rochelle too, when she was here. We had a good team. I was proud of that. The salon had been getting quite a buzz as being the top salon in the Detroit area. And I didn't take for granted that without my team and their efforts this would not be possible. Hood had even suggested I think about opening up another salon somewhere else. But I just wasn't sure if I was ready for that yet. My personal life needed to be a little more stable first.

"Ok, I'm going back to gear up for Leslie, she should be here soon. Just send her right back when she arrives."

No sooner than I sat my blood red Coach bag down on the floor and turned on my curling iron set, Leslie popped through the door.

"What's up, chic?" Leslie spoke as she glided across the floor and landed right in my chair.

"Shit, girl. Ready to lay your wig to the side." I meant every word; doing hair always helped me relax.

"I hope so because I need it. I been so busy I couldn't even get in here last week."

Yes, Leslie was one of those weekly clients. And she didn't look for a discount just because we were cool. I despised people like that. She paid full price to keep herself looking fabulous.

"I know with your new dating life and all," I joked.

Leslie had recently met someone who kept a smile on her face. She kept his identity a secret though. She had never brought him around.

"Oh, no, he ain't the reason. I'm talking about the things I been dealing with period. Things just been crazy, but it's all good though. I'm getting it together. What about you?"

"The same old thing, coming up in here daily and gettin' it in. I been helping out with Rochelle's clients so I have been super busy. It's all good though because that's what we do, have each other's back."

Leslie shook her head in agreement. "I feel you. How is Rochelle doing? It's been a minute since you said anything."

"She a'ight, just gettin' lots of rest. I went by her crib today before I came in. You know Rochelle, she can't wait to get back to this salon. But I told her to chill. She don't need to be in a rush."

"And you are right, she needs to grieve first. If she grieves properly, she will heal a lot faster," Leslie advised.

We had both dealt with the death of a loved one, so we knew what Rochelle was going through. But on the other hand, I worried about her even more because it had only been a short two years since she had lost Lil Lo. And I knew that she still suffered from that because he was the love of her life. Todd's death just added to the devastating pain that she was still trying to suppress.

Before I could make any more comments, my phone started to ring. The ringtone told me that it was my mom. Normally when I'm doing hair and my phone rings I don't answer it. But not only did she call me once, she hung up and called right back. That told me I needed to answer. I paused for a minute to dry off my wet hands, reached for the phone, and hit the talk button.

"What's up, Ma?"

"Mya," she all but screamed through the phone. "What took you so long to answer?"

"I'm at the salon doing hair."

She should have known that. I'm always at the salon.

"I don't mean to interrupt, but I called to let you know he can come home today. They are releasing him tonight."

I almost asked who she was talking about, but when she said "they are releasing him," I knew without a doubt she was talking about Dad. My hands started to tremble. I had been waiting a long time to hear this news. I didn't even know how to respond. Words would not come. The cat had my tongue, as they say. My heart and soul screamed with happiness.

"Mya," Ma screamed my name through the phone again. Matter of fact, she screamed so loud that Leslie heard her. I guess it took me too long to respond to the news.

"Is everything ok?" Leslie asked, making eye contact with me.

"I hear you, Ma." I spoke through choked-back tears. "Just a little shocked."

"I know baby, me too. All of our prayers have been answered. I haven't been able to tell Monica yet, though. She is in class and has her phone off, but she'll be here in about an hour. So I will tell her then."

I knew Monica would cry. She was sensitive that way.

"Ok, ummm what time do we need to be there to pick him up?"

"They just said tonight. You know he has to be processed out and that can take a while. But I don't want him to have to wait around one minute after he is released. So as soon as you get done there, call me. I want you guys to pick him up. I'll wait here."

That was real talk. I understood where she was coming from.

"For real! He won't have to wait. Soon as I'm done, I'll hit you up," I agreed then ended the call.

Leslie's eyes were glued to me. I had told her all about my dad being in prison, so I was sure she had some idea what we were talking about.

"Ok, what the hell is going on?" She held her head up and water dripped down the back of her smock.

"My dad is coming home today."

The words sounded strange rolling off my tongue. I had held my breath for six and a half years not knowing if this would ever happen. I had prayed for this at least a million times.

"That is awesome, Mya." Leslie smiled and leaned back into the sink.

"Ohh wait, I need to call Hood."

As if he read my mind, his ringtone chimed in on my phone. Before long, I was spilling the good news to him. After a little planning, we concluded that we would head down when I was finished up at the salon. We would wait together until they released him through those prison gates. I had waited long enough. I was ready to hold my dad. If this was a dream, whoever pinched me first would get the shit slapped out of them.

DON'T MISS

Baby, You're the Best

by Mary B. Morrison

New York Times best-selling author Mary B. Morrison introduces her most seductive and vulnerable characters yet with the Crystal women, a family whose bonds are tested by love, lust, and the elusive quest for true happiness...

And coming in December 2015

Games Women Play

by Zaire Crown

Tuesday Knight is eager for a better way of life. That means getting out of the game her gentleman's club has been fronting. Her all-female "business" team has made a fortune using the club to attract, seduce—and rob—wealthy men. But in addition to being squeezed by a corrupt cop, an unfortunate incident has put Tuesday deep in debt to a ruthless gun dealer and is creating dangerous dissent behind the scenes...

Turn the page for an excerpt from these thrilling novels...

From *Baby, You're the Best*

Prologue

Alexis

"Thanks for everything. I enjoyed serving you."

You? You? Not this shit again! That bitch waited on us for two hours. I'd kept my mouth shut when the "What would *you* like to drink?" was directed toward my man only. I had to interrupt with my request for a mai tai.

We'd adhered to their protocol by writing our orders on the restaurant's request forms, meaning there was no need to ask what we wanted to eat. The repeat for confirmation, "So you're having the fried wings, rice and gravy, and steamed cabbage and the vegetable plate with double collard greens, and fried okra?" was asked of my man as though he was going to eat it all by himself.

Now that the check was here, I was still invisible? *Aw, hell no!* I pushed back my chair, stood tall on the red-bottom stilettos my man had bought. The hem of my purple halter minidress was wedged in the crack of my sweet chocolate ass but I didn't give a damn. That working-for-tips trick was about to come up short.

I leaned over the table, pointed at the waiter, then said loud enough for all the people on our side of the restaurant to hear, "My man is not interested in you!"

James held my hips, pulled me toward my seat. Refusing to sit, I sprang to my feet, then told him, "No, babe."

Nothing was holding me back from the inconsiderate asshole that obviously needed customer service training. I stepped into the aisle. The only thing separating us was air.

"Not today, Alexis. Please stop," James pleaded.

I extended my middle finger alongside my pointing finger, and my nails stopped inches from the waiter's face when my man reached over the table and grabbed my wrist. I was about to put both of that dude's eyes out.

He posed, one foot slightly in front of the other, tilted his head sideways, put his hand on his hip with a bitch-I-dare-you attitude.

The room was cold. I was heated. The guests became quiet. A woman scrambled for her purse, picked up her toddler, then rushed toward the exit. I didn't give a damn if everybody got the hell out!

"One of these days, sweetheart, I'm not going to be around to intervene," James said. He handed the waiter a hundred-dollar bill.

I snatched it. "Give his ass whatever is on the bill and not a penny more."

James handed that jerk another hundred. This time the waiter got to the money before I did. He stuffed the cash in his black apron pocket, rolled his eyes at me, scanned my guy head to toe, then said, "Thanks. You can come anytime you'd like. Let me get your change."

He stepped back. I moved forward. I didn't have a problem slapping a bitch that deserved it. I swung to lay a palm to the left side of his face. His ass leaned back like he was auditioning for a role in the next *Matrix* movie.

"Don't duck, bitch, you bold. If you feeling some type of way, express yourself." I shoved my hand into my purse.

He screamed, "Manager! Manager!"

I didn't care if he called Jesus. "Say something else to my man. I dare you." If I lifted my gun and put my finger on the trigger, I swear he wouldn't live to disrespect another woman.

James swiftly pulled my arm and purse to his side, then told the waiter, "Sorry, man. Keep the change."

The waiter stared at the guests. "Y'all excuse my sister, she forgot to take her meds." A few people laughed.

"Take your lame-ass jokes to Improv Comedy Club for open mic, bitch. You weren't trying to be center stage before my man tipped you."

"I got you, boo." He pulled out his cell, started pressing on the pad. "You so bad. Stay turnt up until the po-po comes." He turned, then switched his ass away.

James begged, "Sweetheart, let's go."

Some round, short guy with a sagging gut, dressed in a white button-down shirt and cheap black pants, hurried in our direction. "Ma'am. Sir. You need to leave now."

The old lady seated next to our table said, "Honey, you're outnumbered in this town. You gon' wear yourself out."

I told my guy, "Walk in front of me."

Shaking his head, James said, "You a trip," then laughed. "You go first. I have to keep an eye on you."

That was the other way around. Atlanta was a tough place to meet a straight man who cared about being faithful. The ugly guys had a solid five to fifteen females willing to do damn near anything to and for them. The attractive ones had triple those options. The successful, good-looking men with big egos and small dicks were assholes not worth my fucking with. But these dudes boldly disrespecting me by hitting on my man, they were the worst.

"It's not funny, James. I'm sick of this shit."

I knew it wasn't my guy's fault that James was blessed eighty inches toward heaven, one hundred and eighty pounds on the ground with a radiant cinnamon-chocolate complexion that attracted men and women.

James opened the door of his electric-blue Tesla Roadster, waited until I was settled in the passenger seat. He got in, then drove west on Ponce de Leon.

As he merged onto the I-85, he said, "Just because you have

the right to bear arms, sweetheart, doesn't mean you should. I keep telling you to leave the forty at home," he said, laughing. "I'm glad you like my ass."

"Nothing's funny. I don't understand how men hitting on you don't bother you."

"The way you be all up on my ass, what the hell I need a dude for? Soon as you finish your dissertation, I'm signing you up for an anger management course," he said. "You can't keep flashing on men because your father is the ultimate asshole. Let it go, sweetheart."

"That's easy for you to say. Your parents are still happily married. I bet if your dad disowned you, you wouldn't say, 'Let it go.'"

I was still pissed at that waiter. I had to check his ass. I was fed up with dicks disrespecting females. I'd seen my mother give all she had to offer and the only engagement ring ever put on Blake Crystal's finger was the one she'd bought herself.

James held my hand. "You're right, sweetheart. I know how much he's hurt you."

My father, whoever and wherever the fuck he was, was the first male disappointment in my life. Some kids cried because their daddy promised to show up but didn't. Mine never promised. Before I had a first boyfriend, my heart was already shattered into pieces by my dad. Staring out the window, I refused to shed another tear.

Continuing north on Interstate 85, James bypassed exit 86 to my house. "I know how to cheer you up. I'm taking you to Perimeter Mall."

"Thanks, babe," was all I'd said.

I was twenty-six years old and I'd never met my father. My birth certificate listed the father as unknown. Hell yeah, I was angry. My mama didn't fuck herself but in a way she had.

My way of coping with my daddy issues was to not allow any man to penetrate my heart or disrespect me. Every man I dated had to like me more. The second a woman liked a man more than he liked her, she was fucked and screwed.

"Sweetheart, I have a question."

"Don't start that shit with me today, James. Don't go there."

He let go of my hand. "If you answer, I promise, no more questions."

I knew he was lying. He always said that shit and didn't mean it. "What, James?"

"Have you had any other men in your house other than me?"

I could lie. Tell him what he wanted to hear. Or I could tell the truth. Either way it didn't fucking matter! My blood pressure escalated. "I'm not answering that."

He exited the freeway, parked by Maggiano's. "Cool, then I'm not paying your rent this month."

That's why a bitch kept backup.

From *Games Women Play*

The Bounce House was not one of those inflatable castles parents rented for children's parties. It was a small gentleman's club set in a strip mall on 7 Mile with a beauty supply store, a rib joint, an outlet that sold men's clothing, and an unleased space that changed hands every few years. In no way was The Bounce House on the same level as some of the more elite clubs in Detroit; with a maximum capacity of two hundred fifty and limited parking, it would never be a threat to The Coliseum, Cheetah's, or any of the big dogs. It wasn't big but it was comfortable and well managed, plus the owner was very selective in choosing the girls, so this had earned it a small but loyal patronage.

The owner, Tuesday Knight, knew that Mr. Scott, her neighbor and owner of Bo's BBQ, would be waiting in the doorway of his shop the moment her white CTS hit the lot. The old man had a crush on her and always made it his business to be on hand to greet her whenever she pulled in to work.

She frowned when she saw that someone had parked in her spot right in front of The Bounce House. The canary Camaro with the black racing stripes belonged to Brianna, and she was definitely going to check that bitch because she had been warned about that before.

Since all the other slots outside The Bounce, Bo's BBQ, and KiKi's Beauty Supply were taken, she had to park way down in front of the vacant property, and she speculated about which business would spring up there next. In the past five years it had been an ice cream parlor, a cell phone shop, and an occult bookstore. She wished its next incarnation would be as a lady's shoe outlet that sold Louboutins at a discount.

She shrugged the Louis Vuitton bag onto her shoulder then slid out the Cadillac.

Up ahead on the promenade Mr. Scott was standing in front of his carry-out spot pretending to sweep the walk but really waiting for her. This was practically a daily ritual for them.

"Hi, Mr. Scott," she said, beaming a smile.

He did an old-school nod and tip of the hat. "Hey. Miss Tuesday, you sho lookin' mighty fine today." He always called her Miss Tuesday even though it was her first name.

"Thank you, Mr. Scott. You lookin' handsome as always."

He removed his straw Dobb's hat and was fanning himself with it even though the afternoon was mild. "Girl, if I was thirty years younger, I'd show you somethin'!"

"I know you would, Daddy! You have a nice day now, okay."

She strutted by him and since her jeans were particularly tight today, she threw a little something extra in her walk and made the old man howl: "Lord, have mercy!" Mr. Scott was seventy years old and had always been respectful of her and all the dancers so she didn't mind putting on for him. Plus the harmless flirting made his day and got her free rib dinners. When Tuesday reached the door of the club, she turned back to give him another smile and coquettish wave.

What The Bounce House lacked in size it attempted to make up for in taste. There was nothing cheap about the place despite being a small independent establishment. The design wasn't unique: a fifteen-foot bar ran against the far right wall, a large horseshoe-shaped stage dominated the center with twenty or so small circular tables surrounding it, booths were lined against the left wall and wrapped around the front, the entrance was where that front wall and right one intersected, and the deejay booth was next to it.

Before Tuesday had taken over, the entire place was done in a tacky red because the previous owner thought that it was a sexual color. The bar was a bright red Formica that was peeling, the stools and booths were done in cheap red leatherette, the floor was covered in pink and red checkered tile, and the tables wore these hideous black and red tablecloths with tassels that made the place look like a whorehouse from the seventies. Tuesday had brought the place into the new millennium with brushed suede booths, a bar with a granite top, more understated flooring, and mirrored walls that gave the illusion of more space. She even gave it a touch of class and masculinity by adding dark woods, brass, and a touch of plant life.

When she came through the door, the first thing that jumped out at her was that the fifth booth hadn't been bused. There were half a dozen double-shot glasses on the table, an ashtray filled with butts and cigar filters, and a white Styrofoam food container that had most likely come from Bo's. She knew that it was her OCD that caused her to immediately zero in on this but before she could start bitching, one of the servers was already headed to clean it up. Everyone who worked there knew their boss had a thing for neatness so she shot the girl a look that said: *Bitch, you know better!*

Things were slow even for a Monday afternoon. There were only three customers at the bar with eleven more scattered throughout the tables and booths. Most of them were entranced by a dancer named Cupcake who was on stage rolling her hips to a Gucci Mane cut. Two more girls were on the floor giving table dances.

Whenever Tuesday came in, on any shift, her first priority was always to check on the bar. The bartender on duty was a brown-skinned cutie named Ebony who had started out as a dancer then learned she had a knack for pouring drinks. She took a couple classes, became a mixologist and has been working at The Bounce since back in the day when Tuesday was just a dancer.

Ebony called out: "Boss Lady!" when she saw her slip behind the bar.

Tuesday pulled her close so she wouldn't have to compete with the music. "Eb, how we lookin' for the week?"

From the pocket of her apron Ebony whipped out a small

notepad she used for keeping up with the liquor inventory. "What we don't got out here we got in the back. We pretty much straight on everythang, at least as far as makin' it through the week, except we down to our last case of Goose."

Tuesday made a mental note to send Tushie to the distributor. Ebony asked, "How dat nigga A.D. doin'?"

"He all right. Reading every muthafuckin' thang and workin' out. That nigga arms damn near big as Tushie's legs."

"When was the last time you holla'ed at em?"

Tuesday scanned the bar, quietly admiring how neat Ebony kept her workstation. "Nigga called the other day on some horny shit. Talkin' 'bout, 'What kinda panties you got on? What color is they?' " She did a comical impersonation of a man's deep voice. "Nigga kept me on the phone for a hour wantin' me to talk dirty to 'em."

Ebony poured a customer another shot of Silver Patron. "No he didn't!" she said, smiling at Tuesday.

"So I'm tellin' him I'm in a bathtub playin' with my pussy, thinkin' 'bout his big dick. The whole time I'm out at Somerset Mall in Nordstrom's lookin' for a new fit."

"TK, you still crazy!" Ebony was laughing so hard that she fell into her. "The funny part is, he probably knew you was lying and just didn't care."

"Hell yeah, he knew I was lying. A.D. ain't stupid. But when I know that's the type of shit he wanna hear, I always tell 'em somethin' good."

"That nigga been gone for a minute. When he comin' home?"

Tuesday's smile faded a bit. She hated when people asked that question, especially when most of them were already familiar with his situation. A.D. was doing life and a lot of times people asked her when he was coming home just for the sake of gauging her faith and commitment to him. If she said "Soon," she looked stupid when the years stretched on and he didn't show, but if she said "Never!" it looked as if she'd just wrote the nigga off. Her and Ebony had been cool for a long time and she didn't think that the girl was trying to play some type of mind game but the question still bothered her.

As much as she hated being asked about A.D., it happened so often that over the years she had come to patent this perfect response: "He still fighting but that appeal shit takes time." This way she doesn't commit herself to any specific date while still appearing to be optimistic.

Ebony nodded thoughtfully. "Well, next time you holla at 'em, tell that nigga I said keep his head up."

Tuesday left from behind the bar agreeing to relay that message.

She was crossing the room by weaving her way through the maze of tables on the floor when suddenly: *whack!* Somebody smacked her on the ass so hard that it made her flinch.

At first Tuesday thought it was some new customer who didn't yet know who she was, and just as she turned around ready to go H.A.M., she realized that it was her big bouncer DelRay.

DelRay was six foot seven and close to four hundred pounds. He was heavy but didn't look sloppy because it was stretched out by his height. He also knew how to handle himself, possessing a grace and speed rarely seen in men his size. DelRay could be very intimidating when the job required it but by nature was a goofball. While he had the skills to deal with unruly customers physically, he had the game to get most of them out the door without making a scene. This was what Tuesday liked most about him.

She said, "Nigga, I was about to flip!"

"We at four!" he yelled over the music. Lil' Wayne was playing then.

She shook her head. "Hell naw, nigga, we at five!"

He used his thick sausage-like fingers to count. "Two Saturday night, one Sunday before you got in your car, and one just now." He grinned and rubbed his hands together like a little kid eager for a gift. "I get to smack that fat muthafucka six more times!"

"Fuck you!" she said but with a smile. Actually she knew it was only four.

He teased her. "Don't be mad at me, you should be mad at yo boy Lebron! When it get down to crunch-time he always choke."

Tuesday was a diehard Miami Heat fan who swore that she was going to suck Dwyane Wade like a pacifier if she ever met him in person. At the time Miami had the second-best record in the eastern conference so when they came to Auburn Hills to play a struggling Pistons team, dropping a hundred on them seemed like a safe bet. After the Heat lost in overtime, the bouncer asked his boss if he could trade that bill she owed him for the right to smack her on that juicy ass ten times. Tuesday had no interest in fucking DelRay but they were cool like that, so she agreed.

"That's all right though," she fired back. "I still like Miami to win it all. Yo weak-ass Pistons ain't even gone make the playoffs."

"Give us two more years to draft, we gone be back on top again!"

Changing the subject, she asked, "I saw Bree's car out front but is the rest of 'em here?"

DelRay nodded. "Everybody but Tush. Jaye in the locker room skinnin' them bitches on the poker. Bree and Doll in there with her."

"Tush will be here in a minute, I already holla'ed at her. But go tell the rest of them bitches I'm in my office."

"I got you, Boss Lady."

Just as she turned to walk away: *whack!*

She whipped around trying to mug him, but DelRay's fat face made one of those goofy looks that always melted her ice grill. "I'm sorry, Boss Lady, I couldn't help it. You shouldn't have wore that True Religion shit today. You in them muthafuckin' jeans!"

She jerked her fist like she was going to punch him. "Now we at five!"

"You wanna bet back on Miami and Orlando?"

"You ain't said shit, nigga, I ride or die with D. Wade! But if you win this time, goddammit, I'm just gone pay yo heavy-handed ass."

DelRay lumbered off toward an entryway at the left of the stage and parted the beaded curtain that hung over it. That hall had three doors: one for a storage room where all the extra booze and miscellaneous supplies for the bar were kept; the second was the locker room where the dancers changed clothes and spent their downtime in between sets; the third, the door in which the hall terminated, was a fire exit that led to the alley behind the strip mall. DelRay went to the second door, knocked three times, then waited for permission to enter.

An identical hall ran along the opposite side of the stage, only this one did not terminate in a fire door. It was where the restrooms were located, and just beyond them was a door stenciled with the words: *Boss Lady*.

Her office was a modest but tidy space that was only fifteen by twenty feet long. It had a single window with only a view of a garbage-strewn alley. There was a cheap walnut-veneered desk holding a lamp and computer, a small two-drawer file cabinet, two plastic chairs that fronted the desk, and an imitation suede loveseat given to her by a friend. The most expensive thing in the office was her chair: a genuine leather high-back office chair ergonomically designed for perfect lumbar support, costing over fourteen hundred dollars; she had spent more on it than her computer. The office also came with a wall safe that Tuesday never kept any cash in. Other than the above mentioned items, there was nothing else in the way of furniture or decor. Tuesday didn't have anything hanging on the walls and no framed photos were propped on her desk to give it a personal touch. She stepped into her Spartan little space and closed the door.

Tuesday had spent twenty-one years at The Bounce House—ten as a dancer, four as a manager, and seven more as owner—but whenever she came in the office her mind always flashed back to that first time she stepped into it. She was sixteen years old, expelled from all Detroit public schools, a runaway crashing at a different friend's house every night and desperate for money. She had an older cousin named Shameeka who danced there but at the time the place was called Smokin' Joe's. Because Tuesday was light-skinned, pretty with green eyes and a banging body, Shameeka swore she could earn enough money for her own car and crib in no time. So led by her favorite cousin, a young and naive Tuesday was brought in and walked to the door of this office. Shameeka handed her a condom then pushed her inside like a human sacrifice to a sixty-two-year-old bony Polish guy, whose name, ironically, wasn't Joe. There was an eight-minute pound session in which he bent her over the very same desk she still had, then fifteen minutes after that, Tuesday's new name was X-Stacy and she was on the floor giving out lap dances for ten dollars a pop. The old man never asked her age, or anything else, for that matter.

She dropped her bag on the desk and sank into her favorite chair. She thought about what his place had given her, but mostly all that it had taken away.

She was snapped from her reverie when the door swung open. Jaye came in followed by Brianna, and Tuesday immediately cut into her: "Bitch, how many times I got to tell you to stay out my spot?"

Brianna responded with an impudent smirk. "It wasn't like you was using it. Shit, we didn't even know when you was gon' get here."

"The point of havin' my own parking space is so that I'll have a place to park *whenever* I pull up at the club. I don't give a fuck if I'm gone three weeks, when I roll through here, that spot right in front of the door is me! Every bitch who work here know that shit, even the customers know it."

Brianna took a drag off the Newport she was smoking, then flopped down on the loveseat. "Well, you need to put up a sign or somethin'."

"I don't need to put up shit!" Tuesday barked. "The next time I come through and you in my shit I'm a bust every muthafuckin' window you got on that li'l weak-ass Camaro!"

Brianna shrugged nonchalantly and blew out a trail of gray smoke. "And it ain't gone cost me shit if you do. 'Cause like a good neighbor State Farm will be there... with some brand-new windows."

Tuesday pointed a finger at her. "Keep talkin' shit and see if State Farm be there with a new set of teeth!"

Jaye quietly witnessed the exchange with a smile on her face. She took one of the plastic chairs that fronted the desk.

Just then Tushie came in rubbing her ass, with a sour look on her face.

Tuesday laughed. "DelRay got you too, huh? Was it that Miami game?"

She poured herself into the second chair. "Naw, you know fucks wit' dat sexy ass Carmelo Anthony," she said with her heavy southern drawl. "New York let da Celtics blow dem out by twenty."

Tuesday asked, "How many he got left?"

Tushie thought back. "He done got me twice already, he only got three left."

"You only gave that nigga five, he got me for ten! How my shit only worth ten dollars a smack and yours worth twenty?"

Laughing, Jaye said, "Maybe because she got twice as much ass!"

Tuesday shot back at her, "And I still got three times more than you!"

After sharing a laugh, she then said, "We can settle up soon as Doll bring her ass on." Tuesday looked to Brianna. "I thought she was with y'all. Where the fuck she at?"

"How the fuck should I know!" Brianna snapped back at her. "Just because the bitch little don't mean I keep her in my pocket!"

Baby Doll came in as if on cue and closed the door. She snatched the cigarette out of Brianna's mouth, dropped onto the loveseat next to her and began to smoke it.

Brianna said, "Ughh, bitch. I could've just got finished suckin' some dick!"

Baby Doll continued to drag the Newport unfazed. "Knowin' yo stankin' ass, you probably did. Besides, my lips done been in waay worse places than yours."

Baby Doll took a few more puffs then tried to offer it back to

Brianna, who rolled her eyes and looked away. "Bitch, I wish I would."

Tuesday handed her an ashtray. "Well, now that everybody *finally* here, we can take care of this business."

This was the crew: Tuesday, Brianna, Jaye, Tushie, and Baby Doll. Five hustling-ass dime pieces with top-notch game who was out for the bread. Individually they were good but together they were dangerous. These were the girls who played the players.

Tuesday looked at Baby Doll. "You get yo shit up outa there?"

She butted what was left of the Newport and blew the last of the smoke from her nostrils. "The little bit I had being moved today. I only brought *what* I needed for the lick —just enough to make it look like home. It ain't like him and Simone spent a lot of time chillin' at her crib anyway. We either went out or was chillin' at his loft."

Code name: Baby Doll. She was only four feet eleven inches tall with hips and ass that stood out more because of her short stature. Her buttermilk skin always looked soft even without touching it. Delicate doll-like features had earned her name and made her age hard to place: if Doll told a nigga she was thirteen or thirty, he would believe either one. The type of men who typically went for Doll had low self-esteem and loved the ego boost she gave them; her small size and the helplessness they wrongly perceived in her made them feel bigger and stronger while that child-like naiveté she faked so well made them feel smarter. Baby Doll's greatest asset was her bright hazel eyes because she could project an innocence in them that made men want to protect and possess her. It was because of this that, of the five, Baby Doll was second only to Tuesday in having the most niggas propose marriage to her.

Tuesday asked, "What about Tank?"

"He don't think nothin' up," said Doll. "He done spent the last two days blowin' up that phone and leaving texts for Simone. Of course he thinking that li'l situation done scared her off. Same shit every time."

Tuesday nodded. "Good. Text his ass back and break it off. Tell him you thought you could deal with his lifestyle but after what happened you can't see being with him—"

She cut her off. "T.K. I know the routine! I ain't new to this shit."

"Make sure you lose that phone too," Tuesday reminded her. "How did he feel about that loss he took?"

Doll shrugged. "He wasn't really trippin' 'bout the money and he say he got insurance on the truck so he gone get back right off that. He was just so happy that ain't nothin' happen to me."

"That's 'cause you his Tiny Angel!" Jaye said, teasing her. "'All right, I'll open the safe. Just don't hurt my Tiny Angel.'" She did a spot-on impression of Tank's pathetic voice that made them all laugh.

Code name: Jaye. She was five foot nine with a medium build. She wasn't that strapped but her face was pretty as hell; she had dark brown eyes, a cocoa complexion and big full juicy lips that promised pleasure. Jaye was not the stuck-up dime, she was the ultimate fuck buddy. She was that fine-ass homegirl you could hit and still be cool with. Staying laced in Gucci and Prada heels, Jaye was a girly girl but had some special tomboy quality about her that made a nigga want to blow a blunt or chill with her at a Lions game. She was cool, she was funny, and could easily make a mark feel at ease with her sense of humor. Her best asset was her personality but Jaye's secret weapon was her amazing neck game. She sucked dick like a porn star and the same big lips that got her teased in school were now her sexiest feature. Not too many niggas could resist a bad bitch who kept them laughing all day then at night gave them the best head they ever had.

"I know the type of nigga Tank is," said Tuesday. "He gone be suckerstroking real hard about you." She looked at Baby Doll. "Lay low for a while and you might wanna do something different to yo hair. Trust me, this nigga gone be stalkin' you for a minute."

While they spoke, Brianna just quietly shook her head with a look of disgust on her face. "I know having to get next to some off-brand niggas is part of the game, but god damn, Doll, you a better bitch than me. That fat, black, greasy-ass nigga with them big bug eyes; I don't think I could've pulled this one off." She jerked forward pretending to dry-heave then put a hand over her mouth. "How could you look that nigga in the eye and say you love him with a straight face? Just thinkin' about that nigga kissing and touching on me got me ready to throw up."

Doll looked at her sideways. "Bitch, like you said, it's part of the game, that's what we do. I'm playin' his muthafuckin' ass the same way you done had to play niggas and every other bitch in this room. I don't give a fuck what a mark look like, I'm about my paper!"

"Church, bitch!" Tushie leaned over so her and Doll could dap each other.

Brianna leaned back on the loveseat and inspected her freshly polished nails. "Well, I guess I just got higher standards than you bitches."

Code name: Brianna. She was six foot one with the long slender build of a runway model except for her huge 36DD's. Bree had that exotic look that came when you mixed black with some sort of Asian. Like the singer Amerie, she had our peanut butter complexion and thick lips but had inherited their distinctive eyes. Nobody really knew what Brianna was mixed with—Tuesday didn't even think she knew—but whatever she was, the girl was gorgeous. The type of men who were attracted to her were typically looking for a trophy. They liked rare and beautiful things and had no problem with paying for them. Brianna played the high-maintenance girlfriend so well because acting snotty and spoiled wasn't really a stretch.

Tuesday told the girls that they needed to work on their choreography. She felt that it didn't look real enough the other night when Brianna pretended to hit Baby Doll with the gun. "Y'all timing was off. Bree, you looked like you was just tryin' to give her a love tap. And Doll, you looked like you knew it was comin', you was already going down before she could hit you."

Brianna responded the way she typically did to criticism. "Why is you trippin'? The shit was good enough to fool him."

"I'm trippin', bitch, because we can't afford to make mistakes like that. Small shit like that is what could get us knocked."

"Watch this." Tuesday stood up and came from behind her desk. Tushie rose from her seat, knowing that she had a role in the demonstration.

The girls squared off then pretended that they were two hoodrats in the middle of a heated argument: they rolled their necks, put fingers in each other's faces and Tushie improvised some dialogue about Tuesday fucking her man. They pushed each other back and forth, then Tushie gave Tuesday a loud smack that whipped her head around. She held her cheek, looking stunned for a second, then came back with a hard right that dropped Tushie back into her chair.

She fell limp with her head dropped against her chest unconscious, but two seconds later she opened her eyes and smiled. "See, bitches, that's how it's done."

Code name: Tushie. This Louisiana stallion was five foot seven, and while she only had mosquito bites for breasts, her tiny twenty-four-inch waist and fifty-six-inch hips meant she was thicker than Serena Williams on steroids. "Tushie" was the only name that had ever fit her because by thirteen the girl was already so donked up that all her pants had to be tailor-made; by fifteen she was causing so many car accidents from just walking down the street that the police in her small town actually labeled her a danger to the community. Her Hershey-bar skin and black Barbie doll features made her a dime even without being ridiculously strapped. Despite having an ass like two beach balls, Tushie's best asset was really her mind. Many people had been fooled by her deep southern accent but she only talked slow. Tushie knew how to play on those who thought she was just a dumb country bammer and rocked them to sleep. Any nigga thinking she was all booty and no brains would find out the hard way that southerners ain't slow.

Jaye was impressed by the girls' little fight scene. The moves and timing were so perfect that it looked as if they had spent time training with actual Hollywood stuntmen. Jaye was only a foot away from the action, and even though she knew it was fake, she still thought that their blows had made contact. "Wait a minute," she said, curious. "I know she ain't really just slap you but I swear I heard that shit."

"What you heard was this." Tuesday clapped her hand against her meaty thigh. She explained: "Because I'm the one gettin' hit, you lookin' at my face and her hand. You ain't watching my hands! Me and Tush just got this shit down because we been at it longer than y'all."

"Well, I ain't gon' go through all that," Brianna said, standing up to stretch. "Next time I'm just gon' bust a bitch head for real!"

"And now can we wrap up this little meeting so I can get paid and get the fuck outa here. I got shit to do."

Tuesday went into her Louie bag and pulled out a brick of cash. She carefully counted it out into five separate stacks then began to pass out the dividends. As the girls took their individual shares, Tuesday could see the disappointment on their faces. They were expecting more and she was too.

She passed two stacks to Doll, who took one then handed the other to Brianna. Bree made a quick count of the cash then dropped the sixty-five hundred onto the loveseat as if it were nothing. "What the fuck is this?"

Tuesday sighed because she knew this was coming and knew it would be from her. "Look, I know it's kinda short. Shit fucked up all the way around. I got twenty for the truck, seventeen for the work, and my mans said I was lucky to get that."

After doing two months of surveillance on Tank, Tuesday had put Baby Doll on him. It took another seven weeks of Doll's sweet manipulation to get everything they needed for the lick: personal information, alarm codes, copies of his house keys, the location of his stash, and a head so far gone that he wouldn't risk Doll's life to protect it. The girls had hoped for a big score but found out that

Tank was not the hustler they thought he was. The scouting report said that he was heavy in the brick game and the team targeted him expecting at least a six-figure payoff, but when they opened fat boy's safe, all he had was forty-two thousand in cash and twenty-four packaged-up ounces of hard. Disappointed, the girls took his Denali even though it wasn't originally part of the plan. They split the cash that night but it was Tuesday's job to slang the truck and dope; now the girls didn't even get what they hoped for that. Minus what was due to their sixth silent partner, almost four months of work had only grossed them a little over thirteen racks apiece—if you factor in the expenses of renting a temporary place for Doll's alter ego Simone and the Pontiac G6 she drove, they actually netted a lot less. The team typically went after bigger fish, and while they only did about five or six of these jobs a year (sometimes having a few going on at once), they were used to making twenty-five to thirty stacks each, so a lick that only pulled seventy-nine total was a bust.

Tuesday leaned back against her desk. "Look, ladies, I know shit ain't really come through how we wanted on this one. That's my bad but I promise we gon' eat right on the next one." She took the blame because as leader of the group the responsibility always fell on her.

Code name: Tuesday aka Boss Lady. Tuesday was light-skinned five foot nine and thick. She didn't have junk like Tushie but her booty was bigger than average and had been turning heads since puberty. Aside from a pretty face and juicy lips, she had cat eyes that shifted from green to gray according to her mood. Tuesday had put this team together and was the brains behind it. She realized when she was just a dancer that clapping her ass all night for a few dollars in tips wouldn't cut it for a bitch who had bills and wanted nice shit. At nineteen she started hitting licks with A.D., and after he went away, she continued on her own. Over time she recruited Tushie, then slowly pulled in the others. Each of these girls had come to The Bounce just as broke and desperate as she was and Tuesday saw something in each of them that made her think they would be a good fit for the team. Tuesday's best asset was her experience. She had years on every other girl in the group and none of them could crawl inside a mark's head better than she could. She gave them all their game and therefore had each of their skills. She knew how to make a read on a nigga and adapt to the type of girl it took to get him. She could play the innocent square better than Doll, the cool homegirl better than Jaye, and the high-maintenance trophy bitch better than Brianna. She could play one role to a tee or blend a few of them together if it was necessary. Her strength was that she was not one-dimensional like the others. For Tuesday, her secret weapon was actually her secret weakness. None of the girls knew she suffered from obsessive-compulsive disorder. Her illness caused her to reorganize things over and over until they were perfect. Her nature to obsess over every little detail did make her a neat freak, but also the ultimate strategist. Tuesday had a way of seeing all the moves ahead of time and putting together air-tight plans that accounted for every problem that might arise.

"He only gave you twenty for the truck, rims and all?" Bree asked with some skepticism in her voice that everybody heard.

Tuesday nodded. "He said he couldn't do no better than that."

"You know that was the new Denali, right? That's at least a fifty-thousand-dollar whip."

Tuesday frowned. "It's a fifty-thousand-dollar whip that's *stolen!* You thank he gone give me sticker price for it?"

Brianna shrugged and studied her nails again. "I don't know. Just seem like you got worked to me. Either that or somethin' wrong with yo math!"

That made Tuesday stand up straight. Every other woman in that room felt the sudden shift in the vibe as her eyes quickly changed from lime-green to icy gray. "Bitch. is you tryin' to say somethin'?"

Bree didn't retreat from her stare. "All I'm sayin' is that we done put in a lot of time for a punk ass thirteen Gs! If you figure it all out we basically got a little over three thousand a month. A bitch can get a job and do better than that!"

"The lick wasn't what I thought it was and I apologized for that." Tuesday inched closer to her. "But when you got to talkin' all this bullshit about my math, I thought you was tryin' to hint at somethin' else. So if you got anythang you wanna get off yo double Ds about that, feel free to speak up!"

Jaye and Doll just sat there silent because they both knew what Brianna had tried to insinuate and knew that Tuesday had peeped it.

Tushie was quiet too but she was more alert. She knew Tuesday better than anybody and she knew if Brianna said the wrong thing that Tuesday was going to beat her ass. The girl was just tits on a stick and Tushie figured Tuesday could handle that skinny hoe alone, but Doll and Bree were tight. Jaye fucked with Brianna too even though Tushie didn't know how cool they were. She was getting ready just in case she needed to have Tuesday's back.

The tension that swelled in the room seemed to have distorted time so after a second that felt much longer Brianna tucked her tail by looking away. She snatched up the money and threw the straps to her Fendi bag on her shoulder. "Well, if we ain't got no more business then I'm out." She pushed off the loveseat and started for the door. "Doll, if you wanna ride, you betta come on!"

Just as Baby Doll got up to follow, Tuesday called out to Brianna. She paused to look back just as she grabbed the knob.

"You done got you a li'l Camaro, a couple purses, and some shoes and let that shit go to yo head. You the same broke bitch who pulled up in a busted-ass V-Dub Beetle three years ago beggin' for a job; the same bony bitch who used to be out there on the floor looking all stiff and scared, barely making enough to tip out. I pulled you in, gave you the game, and got you together. Bree, don't forget that you came up fuckin' with me, you ain't make me better."

To that, all Brianna could do was roll her eyes.

"But if you ever decide that you don't like what we doin' in here, that door swing both ways." Tuesday looked around, making eye contact with each of them except Tushie then added, "And that go for everybody!"

"Is you finished?" Brianna tried to redeem herself from getting hoed out earlier by trying her best to look hard again.

Tuesday just waved her off. "Bitch, beat it."

Bree left out the office with Doll right on her heels. Jaye got up too but threw Tuesday a *we're still cool* nod before she dipped.

When Tushie got up and went to the door, it was only to close it behind them. She smiled. "I thought you wuz 'bout to whup dat bitch."

"I was. She did the right thang!" Tuesday went behind her desk and fell back into her chair. "I don't know where this bitch done got all this mouth from lately but she startin' to talk real reckless. If she keep it up, what almost happened today is definitely gone happen soon."

Tuesday dug into the inside pocket of her bag and pulled out a quarter ounce of Kush that was tied in a sandwich bag. She passed the weed to Tushie along with a cigar because her girl rolled tighter than she did.

Of the team, Tushie had been down with her the longest and been through the most shit. Even though she was five years younger, they were tight and if Tuesday were ever asked to name her best friend, there was no one else more deserving of the title.

Back in the early part of '05 that ass had already made Tushie a legend in the New Orleans strip clubs. Magazines like *King* and *BlackMen's* were calling her the new "It girl" and for a while rappers all over the south were clamoring to have her pop that fifty-six-inch donk in their videos. She had milked that little bit of fame into a brand-new house and a S550 Benz until Katrina came along and washed it all away.

Then she found herself living in Detroit and having to start from scratch. Tushie featured in a few clubs and because she still had a strong buzz, she was the most sought-after free agent since LeBron James. All the big gentlemen's clubs were shooting for her and as bad as Tuesday wanted her, she didn't think she had a chance. She quickly learned that this country girl had a sharp business mind, because Tushie agreed to come dance at the struggling little spot that Tuesday had just bought, but only if she made her a partner.

Tuesday was leery at first but it turned out to be the best decision she ever made. When Tuesday took over The Bounce House it was losing money faster than she could earn it, but when Tushie the Tease became a regular featured dancer, all that turned around. She was like a carnival attraction as niggas from as far as New York came to see if she could really walk across the stage with two champagne bottles on her ass and not spill a drop or clap it louder than a .22 pistol. The club was packed like sardines whenever she performed, and within months The Bounce House was turning a decent profit. Tushie kept the place jumping for five years, until she finally hung up her thong and retired from the stage.

Singlehandedly saving the club made her a good business partner but years of loyalty and her down-ass ways made Tushie a good friend. Tuesday trusted her so much that she put her up on how they could make some real money together: by robbing niggas who couldn't report the losses.

Tushie finished rolling the blunt, lit it, and took her first three hits. She was passing it across the desk to Tuesday when she spoke in a voice strained from the smoke in her lungs: "I already know you gon' talk to Dres 'bout dis shit."

Tuesday accepted the weed with a nod. "Hell yeah," she said in between puffs. "I'm on my way to do that soon as I leave here. I'm damn sure 'bout to find out why he sent us on this dummy mission."